Mind Searching

Francis B. Nyamnjoh

Langaa

i

Publisher:
Langaa Research and Publishing Common Initiative Group
P.O. Box 902 Mankon
Bamenda
North West Province
Cameroon
Contact Address:
Langaagrp@gmail.com
Langaa_grp@yahoo.com

ISBN: 9956-558-04-4

First Published 1991 by

Kucena Damian Nigeria Limited

AUTHOR'S BIOGRAPHICAL NOTE

 Francis B. Nyamnjoh is Head of Publications and Dissemination with the Council for the Development of Social Science Research in Africa (CODESRIA). He has taught sociology, anthropology and communication studies at universities in Cameroon, Botswana and South Africa, and has researched and written extensively on Cameroon and Botswana, where he was awarded the "Senior Arts Researcher of the Year" prize for 2003. His most recent books include *Negotiating an Anglophone Identity* (Brill, 2003), *Rights and the Politics of Recognition in Africa* (Zed Books, 2004), *Africa's Media, Democracy and the Politics of Belonging* (Zed Books, 2005), *Insiders and Outsiders: Citizenship and Xenophobia in Contemporary Southern Africa* (CODESRIA/ZED Books, 2006). Dr Nyamnjoh has published widely on globalisation, citizenship, media and the politics of identity in Africa. His other works of fiction include *The Disillusioned African*, *A Nose for Money*, *Stories from Abakwa*, and *The Convert*.

CHAPTERS

PART ONE

1

Today, I find myself, strangely, going to the church again. What a long period of absence it's been! What are the more regular church-goers going to think of me? A stranger in paradise for sure. A confirmed henchman of the devil. Satan incarnate! What a world we live in; what manner of judgment! They wouldn't even try to investigate. It is not in their nature. Their ability to seek the truth has been crippled and overshadowed by prejudice and conceit.

Who would believe it anyway, who would believe my story? How can anyone believe me when they have all along been taught to expect Truth only from the palaces of the very great, and never to look down to the slums whence nothing but Falsehood emanates? They would all say I'm kidding, that I'm crazy if I tell them. "How can that be true! How can he blaspheme our Lord in this manner! Could God have done it to a sinner like him? Could the Almighty have chosen such a commoner for so noble a cause? Impossible! If Dr T, Mrs S, Prof. N, or the Honourable Vice Minister tells us of any such vision, we would believe them for their spiritual uprightness, their fathomless faith. We know that they attend the First Mass every Sunday despite their onerous duties; they contribute heavily and donate generously; and they are open handed with friend and foe. But not a Chameleon like Judascious Fanda Yanda to whom the church is what the streets are to beggars. Surely not a nonentity like him! Never!"

Yes, that is how I would be denounced if I dared to tell them of my meeting with God. They wouldn't believe that God, 'their God', is proposing using me to save the people from total frustration. I doubt whether they would even admit they are frustrated. They don't see themselves as belittled and manipulated by anyone, not even by Dr T, Mrs S, Prof. N, or the Honourable Vice Minister. What a pity! They have been trained to lie to themselves and to the world around them. They have learnt to wear masks for convenience, but whose convenience? So I decide to say nothing to anyone, but simply await the time when the Almighty will finally entrust his divine mission into my hands. Only then will I blaze with zeal and vigour like an oil-tanker in the Gulf, devastating falsehood and unmasking the world.

The peremptory words might clatter from the skies when I least expect them; when I'm least ready to act upon them. But I will do my utmost to remain firmly at God's disposal. And I plan to set out without any prior preparations. It would suffice to hear a command like this: "Judascious Fanda Yanda,

I the Lord thy God, beseech thee to come forth and serve my cause. Get thee into the world and destroy all those disciples of the devil who pretend to speak in my name. Also destroy the massive exploitation of mankind and deplore indiscriminate self-aggrandizement. Do this in the name of the Holy Trinity." Yes, I shall take a preliminary sword of words and disappear into the whole wide world, searching everywhere, until all the enemies of good are traced and eliminated. Every society and every generation has its Pharoahs and its Moseses. I'm glad to be called upon to serve my society and generation; and like Moses I would free the wretched of the earth from the whims and caprices of modern Pharoahs. May the Lord be praised.

Once inside the church, I will choose a seat at the very back. I hate to have all those judging eyes piercing my back. I know them well, all those people who attend the services every Sunday. I hate to call them zealots, but that is exactly what they are. "My goodness, even if it were true, what right have they to say that some men come to church not to worship, but to honour their appointments with young women?" I recalled saying this to myself, when last I was here. A daring group of elderly women had gone up to the altar after mass and denounced waywardness amongst the males of the church. Of course, they said there were some exceptions, and even though they failed to call names, everyone knew who their saints were, even easier to guess as Mrs S was one of the women who complained. By the way, who was God to deny those Peter had elected here on Earth? The women had chosen to exonerate Dr T, Prof. N and the Honourable Vice Minister from their list of supposed lechers, and God should see it as such.

The congregation of this church is very susceptible. Its members are easily disturbed and distracted; most allergic to secular noise. The faintest sound by the shoes of a latecomer is enough to attract all eyes upon the latter. A coughing grandmother, a snoring parishioner making up for a sleepless night, or a crying child are centres of attraction. Many were the times when our former Priest Le Père Jean Mouton was irritated by what he termed "the perpetual sheepishness of my congregation".

I remember one vivid incident a couple of years ago. That was barely a month after Le Père Jean Mouton had bought himself a new car, with money pooled by his parishioners. I have never forgiven myself ever since for not having been rich enough to contribute even a widow's mite, and above all for failing to show penitence. But if God really cares for rich and poor as the Bible says, so should His priest! But why then have I not been able to free myself of this feeling of guilt? I don't know. But à nos moutons, or back to our story.

A certain Dr B, intellectual and senior lecturer in the Department of Sociology in the Faculty of Arts and Social Thought, was present in church that fateful Sunday when Le Père Jean Mouton complained that Christians did not participate fully in the mass because, like sheep, they were easily carried away by any triviality. Annoyed, the intellectual, who according to church records was the only rich parishioner not to have contributed towards buying the Priest's car, retorted that Christianity would have no root in Africa today, if the Africans weren't carried away by every passing wind. He quoted figures to show that Christianity was dying in Europe, and to question its relevance in Africa. The Priest was furious; more so because the whole church reverberated with laughter. He abandoned the mass half way and came down to battle it out with the sociologist. He was an aggressive man whose priestly competence many a clearheaded parishioner had come to doubt, covertly.

But as a master of society, the sociologist never waited for the white man to reach him. He walked out of the church, reiterating his assertion: "No sheep, no altar". Too angry to continue the mass, Le Père Jean Mouton sent all of us home, and went for a drive on the outskirts of the city to calm his nerves and plan his revenge. But his Bishop was faster. Three weeks after, we were very happy to learn of his transfer to the Moslem city of Garoua, where there were few readymade Christians like us, but where he could read mass in French, his dear mother tongue. There he intended to start things from scratch, and like a hopeful farmer in the Sahara, he would look forward to a rich harvest once he had sown his seeds.

If there was anything which Le Père Jean Mouton missed in our parish, I'm sure and certain it was his sparkling Renault 18. The car had come to mean so much to him, and who would say he didn't feel bad bidding it farewell? The thought of his successor inheriting the car that had taken so many headaches and so much scheming to obtain, must have pierced his heart like Christ's crown of thorns. I wish him well, who wouldn't?

There are the same old faces; the very church goers of old; today as fervent as ever. For those with cars, I see their rosaries and Hymnals skilfully displayed near the windscreen. The pedestrians are holding theirs out in their hands, feeling proud, complete and endeared. As Christians they have often said that their love for the Lord is boundless, so God's house must constantly be kept warm; not with a physical fire, but with the burning desire to sing, praise and pray collectively. The fire to love and serve should kindle the heart of any true Christian, every member of the Roman Catholic Church of Christ. This doctrine has survived both the destruction of colonialism and the authentication of Africa. Perhaps because the African has always been easily carried away by any triviality.

I recognise all these cars that speed past. Why are they in such haste? Scrambling for a place in Heaven, or merely for a seat in a terrestrial place of worship? Why can't any of them express some brotherliness by stopping for me to jump in? Aren't we members of the same club? No! God forbid! I am being unrealistic, a sinner. How can I expect an Honourable Vice Minister, a distinguished member of the central committee of the ruling party, a Doctor of Philosophy, a Director in the Civil Service, a recognised business Spinster, a reputable Widow, a Chief of service or even a chief of bureau to share a car with a pauper? 'Un voeu rien' like myself? Moreover, they are keenly competing for those privileged front seats. Is this implied in the belief that social visibility here on earth guarantees one a place in Heaven? Chinue

Achebe's Onuka once said, the Sun must first shine on those standing before it can shine on those sitting down. If this applies to God as well, then these scramblers may well have a good reason for chasing after those front seats. But then, it also means that some of us are really "Les damnés de la Terre".

To be honest, our church is a very small one with very few seats. I don't know why the parish council didn't vote for basic infrastructural improvements, instead of a car for our former priest. Perhaps the latter had had a big say in the final decision. If the rich parishioners rejoiced at the departure of our aggressive Le Père Jean Mouton, it was because they detested his policies. He had, for instance, introduced a reform that disfavoured them. Unlike previously, the common Christians were no longer expected to stand up until every well-to-do had acquired a seat for himself. In fact, he was extremely lucky that he didn't lose his life over the issue. Threatened and cursed by the affected, Le Père Jean Mouton had remained courageous. He could tolerate anything but inequality amongst blacks. "No monkey is less a monkey than another," he used to say whenever he had a reform to introduce. But then, why did the parish council agree to buy him a car, when he was so much against the majority of its members? In the name of God?

Perhaps it makes much more sense if I consider that the car was bought for the church, and not for Le Père Jean Mouton as a person. For when he had to go, he was prevented from taking the car away with him.

It has started to drizzle. Soon the narrow peripheral streets in these forgotten parts of the city will become too slippery for both cars and pedestrians. Then people will either give up coming to church today or will have to go somewhere else with good roads, but at the risk of not understanding the language of the mass. Thank God that I have reached Nsam. Some three hundred metres away is the church. I will try to run the rest of the distance in order to avoid being soaked. I have never ceased to wonder why the only church in this great capital city where mass is said in English should be situated at the periphery. Yet, all those who attend mass here come from the bustling centre where the Cathedral towers monumentally next to the splendid L'Hotel Charles de Gaulle. What a splendid juxtaposition too! How I would love to attend mass at the Cathedral, just to know how it feels to be great! But most unfortunately I don't have a good command of French and Ewondo, the principal languages of the city's Cathedral. I must talk to the city's Bishop, if His Lordship will condescend to meet me. Nothing is impossible with me, and nothing should be anyway! If the Bishop's problem is the English language, all he needs to do is pray to God for the gift of tongues. Don't I hear that there is a new breed of Christians who claim to excel in this gift of tongues? He should go to them for advice on how to go about it. We all need fair play in the keen competition for heavenly glory. Everyone ought to take note of that!

Nsam is twenty kilometres away from Briqueterie, the quarter in which I live. Normally I take the bus. But today I am trekking because I haven't any money. Yesterday I lost all my money to those employees of the government bus company known as AVOC. I wasn't aware of the latest of their ever rising fares, when I took the bus for Mimboman. I bought a ticket for 50 francs and squeezed myself into the over-crowded, suffocating French made giant millipede. Once we had gone beyond the Central Post Office, the ticket control officers of AVOC began to conduct a search. They arrested me for buying a less expensive ticket. Despite my efforts to explain, they beat me and took 500 francs, the only money I had on me. Then they abandoned me. I was furious with them for failing to listen. I had desperately tried to make them understand that I couldn't have learnt of their latest fares otherwise; at least not by means of the radio, because I hadn't one, nor through the papers, because these were a luxury I simply couldn't afford. But they would not listen to me; instead they accused me of trying to defraud a public company, as if to say, I and my likes are responsible for the staggering performance of their company. I think they ought to seek the real reasons for their failure, rather than chase after red herrings. Unable to continue with my journey, I had to walk back home.

I arrive at the church at 8.30 a.m. It is an ugly triangular structure. Little care and effort were taken to set it up. I hate to think of it as a triangle because this reminds me of Cameroon. But whereas Cameroon is said to be Africa in miniature, to be a melting pot of cultural, colonial and linguistic diversities, the triangle of Nsam is at best a delusive attempt to save a fading identity. It is like a life-supporting machine set up in order to give false hope to the relations of a dying person. I have always wondered why people should exhibit such impatience in matters of religion. That is like believing in God with some reservations; which is to say, being a tentative Christian. May God forgive many such mistakes, for the spirit is willing but the flesh is weak.

Of course, all seats are occupied! There is hardly even a standing space. The church is as full as it was when I attended it last. Perhaps this is the way it has been since then. Which might mean that nobody has missed me. Could that really be true? Could it be true that even the Priest failed to notice the hole my absence must have created in his congregation? No, that isn't possible; I'm not all that insignificant. I know almost everyone who attends mass here. Half of them I even know by their Christian names. They also know me; I am sure about that. My absence hasn't been such that they should easily forget me. Even the Honourable Vice Minister surprised me once in town. He was driving himself that day as if to tell onlookers that it is for sheer prestige that he has a chauffeur at all. Watching the car as it wrestled along the history-making streets of Briqueterie, I thought he wasn't doing badly. He could well drive himself to work and back everyday, only the feeling of grandeur wouldn't let him. He brought his Mercedes 280 SE to a stop on spotting me in front of Le Cinema du Pays, 'The Local Centre for Training Juvenile Delinquents', so would some call it. He called me by name and asked me what I was doing there. I pointed at the posters, and he understood and smiled at me. "A nice film, eh?" he said, half question and half statement. I simply nodded, with an attitude of so-what?, although I wasn't remorseful in the least, about the fact that his children would never be seen by the general public as delinquents, not because they weren't necessarily that, but because they watched their own violent films secretly at home on the video. He took out his wallet and handed me 2000 francs from it. It's hard to describe the way I felt. I doubt if the feeling would have been different if God himself had called me by name.

However, when he had driven off and my head was clearer, I started cursing myself for accepting his gift. I was anxious to know why he had given me the money. Was it out of pity for a miserable and destitute delinquent? Was it a sign of Christly brotherliness, or was it just an over rich man disposing of superfluous wealth? I hate those who give in order to ridicule or to show their superiority. There are those who give without strings from whom I like taking. But just how possible is it to find someone who gives without attaching strings? Couldn't one argue convincingly that even a gift by one's own parents is selfishly motivated? Who is the father primarily thinking of when he sends his son to college with the hope that the latter can eventually support him and the rest of the family? Politicians behave in the same way towards the very people whose interests are supposed to be their primary concern.

What would one say of a President whose argument against democracy is that too much of it would oust him from power? Of course, he might never be as blunt as that but the fact reminds that in his heart of hearts all his public rationalisations are reducible to that. Persistent frustration by others has made me conclude that every gift, whatever wrap we use to conceal its true nature, has strings attached to it. Since I discovered this bitter truth, I never take a bottle of beer from a friend which I am not sure of repaying. This is the same attitude I hear people have in the West, where civilisation is said to be centuries ahead of what we have here. I congratulate myself for personally discovering what the white man discovered ages ago, that every gift is an investment of some sort, a moral cord tired around the conscience of the receiver by he who gives. That is the power of the gift, a psychological power.

Whenever I come late to church, I never cease wondering what would happen if I were equally too late for a seat in Heaven. Would the Almighty let me stand eternally, or would He do his best to find me a seat? I sometimes amuse myself to think that Le Père Jean Mouton would seat me, if he happened to be there with God, thanks to his policy of no monkey being less a monkey than another. But generally, I always console myself with the belief that the heavenly mansions and seats are as infinite as they are comfortable. Didn't Jesus say that there is room enough for each and everyone of us in his father's house? But what a price we have to pay just to get there! I wonder what they have in store there that Dr T, Mrs S, Prof. N, and the Honourable Vice Minister haven't already had here on earth! Perhaps Jesus was right when he said that the Kingdom of Heaven was for the poor.

It still drizzles outside. My T-shirt is somewhat wet. I look around me, others are equally wet. Even those with cars have to park them some distance away and walk to this ugly triangle. Which makes the drizzle appear like a compulsory blessing for all of us: rich and poor, high and low, adult and youth, man and woman, worshippers and persons on rendezvous. In which case, the church is comparable to Heaven where none can choose to go with his limousines and mansions. Heaven, having a superfluity of such luxuries already.

Many a story has been told about the LAST DAY. Stories that frighten rather than appeal. Sometimes I feel there is a quality the church badly lacks. Instead of learning how to persuade or appeal to the mind, its authorities have always sought to achieve their mission by instilling fear. The Bible itself is a book of FEAR, that threatens us with punishment if we fail to behave in a prescribed way. Often I wonder about God's idea of democracy. Are the Angels allowed to freely express their love and allegiance, or are they compelled to do so? We are told that Lucifer had to be chastised for showing an unwanted degree of ambition. The question is: What makes the ambition unwanted, and who brands it thus? Isn't it democratically believed that a child might attain greater heights than his parents ever dreamt of in their life time? Or that a student might grow to be more authoritative than his master? Then why all the fuss and double-standards?

Two weeks ago at Le Cinema du Pays, I watched 'The Warrior', a film depicting Dutch colonialism in Asia, and an episode made me change the picture I had interiorised about the white man. Before then I thought all whites think alike and in a unilinear manner too; that they all enjoyed seeing other races suffer. And I had evidence in support of my collective condemnation of whites. Hadn't these whites for hundreds of years tethered blacks to the inhuman pole of slavery? Hasn't the whole world borne Europe's hegemony and chauvinism at one point or another in history? Aren't South African blacks presently contesting the biblical idea of a greater Hell because of the odious policy of apartheid perpetuated by a handful of white sadists? And aren't these sadists encouraged by countries where it once was an unpardonable crime to whisper "good day" to such a monkey as a black man? But how struck was I when the daughter of the Dutch Governor-General in the film blatantly opposed her father and the idea of colonial domination! And though her father molested and threatened to kill her, Maria (as she was known) remained adamant. My admiration for whites like Maria is boundless. But how many of such are still left in the world? For most unfortunately, Maria, because of her revolutionary ideas, was killed in the film! She was the victim of her reactionary father, the epitome of a world madly at war with alternative perspectives.

Can parents learn from Maria's experience? If they could I would be more than happy. Parents should know and accept that children are free to think and do as they please. Let them take time to reflect on how disastrous it would be to the world as a whole if people all had to think in the same way if children were literally forced to perceive the world through the squinting retinas of their aging parents. The idea of change would be killed. Imagine what that entails! It means that sinners would perish as sinners; the Third World would remain Third

World forever; and it also means that once poor never rich; and above all that South African Blacks would continue to swim in the gloomy pool of apartheid; and last of all, it means that Africans would continue to bear the yoke of perennial dictatorships and the caprices of nitwitted leaders. No! Democracy is good because it encourages tolerance which makes change possible. How I wish parents and patrons the world over could but understand this truism!

The walls of the church are covered with cobwebs; they were covered in the same way when I visited it last. The wood used to make the roof is being daily transformed into sawdust, some of which keeps falling over our heads, because the church still has no ceiling. Everything here always seems rather patched up. Nothing ever seems to get its deserved attention. Why all the

half-heartedness? Communion shortages are commonplace occurrences here! Yet I'm told by members of congregation who matter that Communion can now be made in Cameroon, although the wheat and wine continue to be imported from France. In as much as I appreciate France's strategic importance to the wellbeing of Christians here in Cameroon, I wonder why the French aren't selling us enough wheat. I don't want to be told that this church of ours is feeling the financial pinch already. Who is the Christian that likes to share his little piece of The-Body-Of-Christ with others? Perhaps the clerics don't know that some of us live by this bread alone?

I pity that lady who did the first reading. Why did she choose to disgrace herself in that way? We all know her very well. Everyone knows for instance that she has never ventured out of Cameroon, let alone having gone to America. But here she is bleating like a goat in an effort to read like an American. What a contradictory place the world is! What an irony! When the Americans are busy doing all they can to abandon the idiosyncrasy of speaking incomprehensibly like people with burning coal in their mouths, there are Cameroonians like this young lady who would do all to pick it up. I know what she is suffering from, a strange disease called Ameromania, a chronic stage of the psychoses generally referred to as Occidenomania. I only wish she finds a cure for it soon enough!

On the other hand, the second reader was as natural as one would expert of an authentic Cameroonian. She didn't set out to mimic anyone, but was simply herself, playing no tricks with her voice. She had no airs either, and was quite normal in her speed. I like her for that. May God bless the man with whom she had her daughter whom she brings to church every Sunday. I know so much about her, as I do of many other people in the church. There is a lot of gossiping before and after mass every Sunday; whoever has a keen ear knows a lot about others and their affairs and concerns. This particular lady for instance, is in every one's heart. To some she is a heroine, while to others she is a victim. It depends from what angle one looks at her. In any case, the fact about her is that her would-be husband went to Europe where he fell in love with a white woman and subsequently refused to return home. When she finally learnt of it, she felt bitter and lonely. She had her daughter, but refused to marry the child's father because the latter was a drunkard. He used to take three crates of beer everyday, Sundays inclusive, and never went to church. A year after the child was delivered however, its unfortunate father died, poisoned by alcohol, and rattled by domestic problems. This lady and her daughter have offered mass for the dead man every month since.

The Gospel was well read by Rev. Father Limbo the priest who took over from Le Père Jean Mouton. Priests are good readers. Reading well is part of their training. But the sermon was dull as usual. How these Priests love to paraphrase the Bible in the name of preaching. If that is all one should hear in church, then I really don't have to regret my absence. Paraphrases are not what anybody wants. If only priests would learn how to preach from Protestant Ministers. The latter are on the average better preachers, by every standard. Yet priests spend far more years as seminarians. What do they learn to do for seven years? Probably learning how to lie to themselves and to others, to deny what is there, and to dissemble; yes, seven years spent trying one mask after the other, to see which best fits them in their dubious role as spiritual mentors. A strange thing to do without compunction!

Yet there must be a secret somewhere. Perhaps the Protestant Ministers preach well because they are protesting. They are like the opposition in politics, in states where such opposition is tolerated of course and everyone understands just how difficult a task it is to oppose. It is said that the opposition never wins elections, but that governments lose them. Perhaps these priests do actually know how to preach, but simply choose to do what they do for the sake of safeguarding the mediocre traditions of their church. Thus in a way, sacrificing the Gospel in order to save the Church. They would rather tell half truths and keep their flock intact, than tell the whole truth and lose their dominions. Were Christ suddenly to return to Earth, I wonder if he would accept the church whose keys he handed over to Peter the Rock before retiring to his Father's Kingdom. Much has changed, but little has changed for the better. Perhaps my divine mission will turn out to be all about giving the church new vitality, and re-shaping it to answer more to the rising aspirations of the long forsaken majority, than to the inordinate ambitions of a few politically minded dissemblers. I look forward to God's call with joyous expectancy. When it finally comes, I shall stand on the house tops and proclaim the new religious, social, political and economic order, inviting all and sundry to join in making the world a just and better place to live.

I feel like kneeling down and praying to God just now, in my own way telling Him how uplifted I feel to have been chosen as the standard bearer for the crusade against all sorts of misdeeds perpetuated in His name, in the name of His people, and in the name of Peace and Justice. But the church is so crowded that it is simply impossible for me to kneel down. I know what to do. I'll just bend down my head and murmur a few words of prayer. It doesn't really matter how or where one prays, does it? The important thing is the intention. The rich man who prays in the sumptuous comfort of his exuberant mansion, is no nearer to Heaven than the starving youth in the overcrowded filth and misery of the slums, muttering words of prayer to God for courage to steal some food in order to sustain his feeble body. Just as the rich man isn't necessarily more drunk because he drinks champagne from France than his poor counterpart who can only afford palm wine from the village.

I have been wondering why the 'Big People' of our time cannot set the pace for others to follow. At secular meetings it is the commoner who comes first, not the car owners. "Sorry to be late. I was caught up here, I was caught up there," or, "The traffic was heavy, blah, blah, blah ..." The reasons they give are invariably the same. But why is it invariably the better off that come late to meetings? In church the situation is the same, where it would appear the very big either take exceedingly heavy breakfasts, or take so long to beautify themselves and to dress up. One such chronic late comer is the Honourable Vice-Minister. Today he is as late as ever.

Where does he think himself, the Honourable V.M? Some people call him V.M, while others prefer to call him Minister but it is clear that he loves to be addressed simply as the Honourable Minister. The church is definitely not his house where he can walk in and out as he pleases, nor his Vice-Ministry, where I hear he has the daily privilege to be two hours late for work. At this rate I think the next thing he will do is to stage an unsuccessful coup d'état against God! You may laugh, but that is it. If not, how do you explain the fact that the Honourable Vice-Minister has never, as far as I know, come to church before the Gospel? Isn't that the characteristic disrespect that usually precedes and predicts inordinate ambition? One might even conjecture that he privileges the offertory. For that is always when he walks in, full of dignity and authority. Even then he makes sure he is the last person to go up to the altar. Several times I have caught our new priest Rev. Father Limbo red-handed, smiling to the Honourable Vice-Minister instead of concentrating on the mass.

How the Honourable V.M came to know me is a little bizarre. It was a long time ago. It was at mass, and he thought himself the very last person for offertory that Sunday. But just when he was about to regain his privileged seat, I came up to throw my widow's mite beside his thousands. Even Rev. Father Limbo seemed to despise what I did that day, judging from the scornful look he gave me. As for the Honourable V.M, he sent his bodyguards who were gendarmes to call for me after church. The service over, I was arrested, literally arrested, and brought before him. He looked at me spitefully for a minute or so, then reproached me for disrespecting the natural order of things. He warned me sternly and took down my name. Yes, he took it down in his Black Book which meant that thenceforth, I was to be perceived and treated as an enemy, a subversive element in the political system in which he headed a Vice-Ministry. I had read in the foreign papers smuggled into Briqueterie from neighbouring countries about those tormented and tortured victims. That evening I locked myself in my dark little room in the heart of Briqueterie, "Le Quartier du bas fond", and prayed to God for instant forgiveness. I cursed myself for having dared to offend the Honourable V.M. "It must have been the Devil," I whispered. "Yes, the most vile Devil must have led me up the garden path." I cursed and denounced Satan more than ever before. Even before I had finished praying, I could feel God's peace and grace flow through my veins, giving me the reassurance I needed so badly. I felt happy, really happy to be forgiven.

Yes, today the Honourable V.M is as late as ever. He comes again after the Gospel. His gendarmes escort him in front of the church where he takes his privileged seat, one specially reserved for him. Then they withdraw to wait for any eventuality at the back of the church where I stand. Whenever I see these two gendarmes, I never cease to chuckle. They are huge, muscular, tall and imposing, like people who have spent all their lives eating garri and cocoyams, weightlifting and body-building. I believe they are trained to look as imposing as possible. The Honourable V.M on his part is diminutive and weak, an extremely little man who puts on extra shirts and jackets to look bigger and more daunting. Some people even think it is because he is physically so vulnerable that he exaggerates the presence of his thugs. I don't share this point of view. Rather, I believe that it is because becoming a member of government is such a rare, difficult and competitive phenomenon that the Ministers and Vice-Ministers are so well guarded. Loyalty isn't a very common gift in heterogeneous societies, and no President wants to lose the few disciples who agree with him over the size of the national cake, and how this cake ought to be shared out. That to me is the reason why ministers are so heavily guarded.

I don't understate when I say that becoming minister is difficult and competitive. It is said that whenever a cabinet reshuffle is about to take place, there is real euphoria amongst potential candidates. Since one of the major criteria for selection is ethnicity, ministers-to-be know just whom to fight if they must be appointed. It is time for them either to criticise their kinsmen in government - to say how little these have contributed towards the development of the tribe or clan, to defame the character of fellow candidates from the same ethnic group as themselves, or to clamour for a place by waging war against other ethnic groups which appear to have had more than their fair share of the national cake. There is lobbying of every kind in and around the capital city. But there is also the appeal to the supernatural to intervene and influence the outcome.

Usually almost everyone is involved but for quite different reasons - everyone wanting things to turn out his or her own way because of this or that. Cabinet members consult diviners to see if they are likely to conserve their portfolios. If the findings are negative, they make desperate attempts to influence the situation. Some offer sacrifices to appease their ancestors, while others acquire amulets that allegedly render them invulnerable. There are others who are believed to use magical spells on the President, spells that can make him alter his decision at the very last moment. It is rumoured that several cabinet changes have had to be postponed for months or even years for no apparent reason. On many an occasion, the allegation continues, a minister has had to be retained in the government when public opinion would normally have had him out of it. And one may well ask for whose interest these individuals usually fight to stay in power, when the people they are supposed to represent would even pay with their lives to have them replaced? Do they really mean it when they constantly refer to having the national cake equitably distributed? Distributed by whom, with what right, and to whom?

As for aspirants, the struggle for a foothold in the government is equally keen. They do the same things as those already in government, but for a different reason. The real reason is always self-interest, but no one is actually ever bold enough to say that's what he or she is fighting for. I would like to see how many of them would stay on in government if they were asked to give up a year's salary in the name of nation-building, their much resounded credo. A nos moutons. The aspirants do all to influence the departure of others in order to be brought in. This means that they will stop at nothing to have things their way, not even murder. Some Cameroonians who think rather too much about the economy have claimed that the reshuffles are the only time when rivers can flow uphill meaning, the only time when money is actually brought into the country from foreign bank accounts, instead of the reverse that happens every other time. Candidates withdraw this money to bribe their way through. It might be slanderous, but certainly not uncommon to hear people say that at such times even the President is sure to make several millions more for himself, millions he bank abroad, the place where money rightly belongs.

There is the famous story of a hopeful who in the 1960s went to consult a marabout about his chances of being admitted into the club of decision makers. By the way, isn't it ironic that a nation should spend time, energy and resources baking a cake for itself, just for this same cake to be abandoned to a handful of ill-chosen and ill-intentioned clowns who haven't the slightest idea what it takes to bake one? Yes, but back to our famous story. The said hopeful went to have his fortunes divined by a marabout. The latter asked him to bring 30 black goats, 15 white cocks and 5 million francs. Just to be minister!, some of us may exclaim, but these aspirants sure know of something we ignore about being minister. There must be a beehive somewhere in that club of theirs that produces honey of exceedingly good quality! The hopeful's goats were all slaughtered and buried along with the money in a mass grave dug at night on the outskirts of the city. The fowls were also slaughtered, but they weren't buried. Instead, their blood was collected and cooked, then it was given to the aspirant to eat everyday until the reshuffle. He sure must have enjoyed it, for blood takes the form of a cake when cooked. On his part the marabout assured the hopeful that he the marabout would finish eating the fowls before the reshuffle. It was necessary that he did that, if his client had to be made minister, he emphasised.

When the reshuffle came and the aspirant was not selected, he went at night to dig the grave and take back his money. He was surprised that both the goats and the money had vanished. "That surely taught him his lesson," one may say, but these people can be highly obstinate. And hypocritical too! It is because in public our famous aspirant professed to be rational and scientific, and decried superstition and magic that he lost his money, goats and fowls. How could this much respected son of Science and Reason suddenly turn around and accuse a marabout for tricking him? When will they learn?, one may well ask with a sigh of pity.

Also, there is a living example of a man who missed becoming minister because he proceeded to celebrate his appointment long before it was officially announced. He was one of the numerous victims of rumour-mongering. In a society where information is as scarce as water in the Sahara, rumour is bound to serve as a double edged sword, to the government and to the governed. Last but not the least, is the foolhardy Doctor of Philosophy, whose name I withhold in the name of peace. He is said to have signed a contract with the Devil that he must serve as minister or die and go to hell. So he spends all his time writing letters to the presidency, denouncing and defaming everybody whom he sees to be standing in his way to greatness.

As early as the late sixties four Christian members of government were known to have accompanied their Moslem counterparts on a pilgrimage to Mecca. There, they won titles that identified them with Islam and Mohammed its founder, and that replaced "God" with "Allah" in their vocabulary. I hear that the President was so pleased with their initiative in the right direction that he decided to make them permanent members of government by declaring them prestigious "Ministers of State" or "Ministres d'États" to be more original and legitimate. This means that the so-called ministers of state have since stopped worrying about their positions and. maybe, ceased visiting the marabouts. I would hesitate to confirm this though, knowing just how fickle they tend to be in matters of faith and principle. To be honest, this story did shock me to the bones when I first heard it. I'm shocked in a similar manner by most stories I hear in this country.

How can men prostitute their dignity just to satisfy inordinate ambitions for loud sounding nothingness? It's a great pity. Quite grievous! Let's suppose, just suppose, that power changes hands one day and a Christian becomes President. I'm quite convinced that Moslems would attend mass and receive Holy Communion if the Pope should pay us a visit. What a scandal! What a shame! To stoop this low just because one fancies the adjective "Honourable" is a great disgrace, something I'd offer my life to avoid doing! Why must some of us strive to please our superiors in such mean ways, if convinced we are that we merit our places, and that these places merit us? The whole problem is a simple and straightforward one. Our nation's tragedy is that the right men are never made to occupy the right places. They are never made to occupy any place at all! We prefer to flirt around with the idea of regional balances in representation as if goodwill doesn't suffice as criterion. The fact that we stress regional and ethnic balances so much in government and high office belies our very sinister, cloudy designs. With such thinking and practices, the cream is forced to watch in passivity the gross mismanagement of the country's affairs by a strange band of mediocre blockheads! To hell with all the brothers, sisters, cousins, uncles, and friends! Why do we always encourage the feeling that it is much easier to talk in terms of tribes, regions and linguistic groupings, than simply of Cameroon and Cameroonians? Are our differences real or faked?

I know many a politician would lynch me, if such thoughts as these were [to be] translated into words and distributed in the form of tracks. But I sense a change, a great change, a change that would rock the corrupt foundation of the country with banners of freedom and peace. Yes, I see a change in the wind, a change for the better. And the sooner it comes the better. Let he who eventually comes up as leader of a New Cameroon be an intellectual - that is to say, a true man of the people. Let him not only promise freedom and abundance, but let him actually deliver the goods. For there are many who promise, but few fulfil. I believe in the rule of clearheaded intellectuals, not muddleheaded nitwits. How often have I heard individuals referred to as 'Les Intellectuels' in public places here and there in this great city? Yet why hasn't any of the lot come up with proposals for a better Cameroon? Are they genuine intellectuals or are they pseudo? Time will tell. May this country be blest in the '80s and thereafter, blest with overdue change. Let the society of rumour, intrigue and dishonesty that was born in the '60s fade away forever.

Do I have a part to play? Is my mission to be in any way connected to this political change? I have no idea, but I'm confident that the Almighty will make it known to me as soon as He deems it necessary. What colossal task will there be for me? I who know nothing in politics?, who am just a nonentity in my country? Who would recognise or listen to me? Certainly not the likes of Dr T, Mrs S, Prof. N, or the Honourable V.M! If I must be leader, it has to be for a totally new type of Cameroonian, the Cameroonian who like myself has lived virtually unseen and unheard. Yes, such is the only person to whom I'm likely to appeal, and who would not question the low level of my education, and the fact that I live nowhere better than Briqueterie. It won't be an easy task, that I know just too well. But I am determined to succeed. So I keep waiting for God's call, reassured by the fact that He is supreme, and that nothing is impossible with Him.

A nos moutons, once more. It is common knowledge that the only time the Honourable

V.M ever goes out without his bodyguards is when he visits spinsters and widows. At such times, not even his driver goes with him. He does the driving himself, stopping here and there to present an ambiguous gift or two to people he never expected to meet. Whatever the case, he remains one of the most respected church-goers amongst the Anglophone Catholics of the capital. "If ministers are corrupt," I've heard apparently intelligent people argue, "The Honourable V.M must be an exception. He goes to church regularly. Do you think he could believe in God and be corrupt at the same time?" Some people claim he is quite popular with the Anglophone community here in the city. He wouldn't be minister if he wasn't, I suppose.

The Honourable V.M has also proven himself to be a competent leader. On several occasions he has complained that the city cathedral has no place for mass in English, despite the fact that "our country is bilingual in English and in French." Unfortunately, the expression of his dissatisfaction has always been misdirected. Deliberately so? That is what some of his critics believe. Some however argue that only a mad fool who grossly ignores the realities of Cameroon would expect the Honourable V.M to behave with integrity. "Isn't he there," they would ask, "to fill his pockets with bits and pieces of the national cake by playing down radical criticisms?" And what is wrong with doing his duty, if duty it is?

It is no longer news to anyone that a couple of weeks ago, a Minister of State did just his duty when he alerted the forces of Law and Order to apprehend a professor in the Department of Contemporary Studies at the National University. The latter, "a disgruntled Bamileke scholar", is believed to have subverted the Government policy of Self-Reliant Development ("Développement Auto-Centré") by insinuating that what was in fact being practised was a sort of Stomach-Centred Development ("Développement Auto-Ventré"). The professor is said to have accused Ministers who tried to justify such corrupt practices with the adage that "A goat can only eat where it is tethered". He argued that his problem wasn't with the eating, but with how much was eaten, and with the fact that certain officials took undue advantage of the abundance that surrounded them. Did it ever occur to them, he asked, that certain goats remained tethered to aridity all their lives? In that case, wasn't it important that each goat should have only its fair share of the national cake? And for being so daring, the professor might never see his family and students again. For rumour holds it that he is imprisoned in a dungeon somewhere in the north of the country, and faces possible execution if the international community fails to clamour strongly enough for his release.

Why did he speak out so bluntly? Why couldn't he have been more tactful? It bothers me to know that some students can be that mean! For the professor is said to have been reported by one of his students – apparently commissioned by the Minister of State to spy on him. What a dirty world, that university of theirs! It's strange what I hear goes on there. Why on earth cannot professors be allowed to do their teaching in peace? Why do you employ someone in the name of national development, yet deny him the scientific right to analyse the national situation? What do you want him to teach? About Europe and America? About everywhere else but Cameroon? Then how shall the latter be developed, if its students know nothing of their own country? No matter how bitter the professor felt, it was unwise to be so blatant in his attack. See what it cost him! Imprisonment, and who knows, perhaps his life.

I for one have decided to be less foolhardy. I may be poor and miserable, but I'm certainly not an ass. I'm mad neither. That is why I have chosen to keep my mind searching exercise an internal mental process. Not until I'm sure and certain that the country is free and democratic enough, that the people have a right to information, and that the authorities are ready to let Truth substitute Rumour, not until then will I vent my thoughts on paper. For now, the only freedom that each and every Cameroonian still has is the Freedom of Thought. Thoughts are the only things that have escaped the diktats of present-day dictators, and I'm pleased to take advantage of them. I wish I had a key into the minds of my fellow country-people. It would be nice to know just how many of them are thinking about change in the same way as I do. How many of them have already ousted the present order in a thousand and one coup d'états planned and executed in their minds only? And how many of them are confident that the team they have chosen to replace the present government would take proper care of their national cake? It would really be a good thing to know how many Cameroonians are having the same waves of consciousness as I do. Unfortunately, I'm just a man. Only the Almighty can reveal minds to me. I'm glad to be his messenger, the standard bearer in a tribal war, armed to the teeth and hiding behind the rocks in the mountains, ready to order my troops to attack just when the time is ripe.

Back to the church. Soon it is communion time. Rev. Father Limbo is assisted by Rev. Sister B. I watch keenly to see if the situation has changed since I was here last. Will the Honourable V.M behave himself for once in his life? He is sitting in front of Sister B and should normally take communion from her. But will he? Of course not! The question is answered even before I finish thinking of it. He stands up, carefully deviates the sister and takes from the priest. Then he makes the sign of the cross and sits down to pray. There are many things about this Honourable V.M that baffle me. First, why does he never kneel down in church? It is true that he dresses himself in expensive white 'ghandura' or in three piece suits. But is that why he should not kneel? He has someone especially employed and paid by the state to clean his dresses for him. So why does he bother? Strange, isn't it?

Second, the Honourable V.M never comes to church with his wife. He says she is peasant and not pleasantly urban. Had he known he might become minister some day, he would certainly have married a more 'modern' woman. I am told he wanted to divorce her immediately after he became V.M, but the President saved the marriage by threatening to retaliate if the V.M went ahead with 'his madness'. Of course, the

Honourable V.M needed no convincing that he would rather have a bush wife than lose his place in the cabinet. At banquets at the presidential palace, where every invitee is expected to come along with his wife, he is said to introduce his wife as "the woman my father forced upon me in the village before I was anything." That is his funeral.

Third, as a matter of habit, the Honourable V.M leaves the church before the last blessings, as if to say he doesn't need them for survival! The congregation murmurs as usual, but what else? He goes away quite unhurt, the murmurs reinforcing his self conceit. What a worthy Christian! May God bless him, his thugs, and his all.

I wonder if anyone is free from the feeling there is something fundamentally wrong with African politicians? This defect is perhaps due to: "the dramatic changes in the continent, provoked by violent exposure to Western values and the attempt to patch up a reconciliation with traditional African values", to quote from a pompous foreign newspaper article I read months ago. How can one believe what I read in another paper some weeks ago! A retired minister, who entered politics during the heyday of primary school teachers and church pastors, wanted to make a dramatic comeback. So he laid down a strategy. Somehow he had come by the state secret that a roving pope was contemplating visiting his East African nation. So he made a desperate effort and was finally selected as one of the readers at a mass to be celebrated at the International Airport of the capital city. But so unfortunately for him, just when he thought he had at last succeeded in impressing his President and making the latter understand he wasn't a subversive, the cardinal found out he was a Protestant and not a Catholic! And so he never read! But he never lived to bear the ignominy. For he immediately selected a good cord and hanged himself behind his mansion. The papers further reported that the Holy Father reproached the cardinal for frustrating the veteran's efforts to do God a service. The President, to heal old wounds with the tribe of the deceased, took political advantage of the episode by organising a state funeral for "a patriot of unequalled service to the nation".

I feel freer with the Honourable V.M's thugs gone. All through the mass they snored as if they slept. Strange thing that they should snore while their eyes stay wide open. Perhaps they actually slept. Of course they should! It is not easy for one to spend all his time watching others. Excessive altruism is no use. But is that really the case? Do these thugs actually love their job? Nothing is less certain!

How often have I heard of guards victimizing their masters? Every passing day furnishes me with more evidence that these thugs are very dissatisfied with their positions.

The first such example is as old as history itself, and occurred in Europe where civilisation is falsely claimed to have been born. I remember it well from books I read at school. It tells the pathetic story of a monarch whose soldiers turned against him at the battle front, just when he was about to do a great deed for himself and his kingdom. He was captured and assassinated by his soldiers through the instigation of the ambitious standard bearer of his army. When the dubious standard bearer was victorious over the enemy troops, he returned home with the falsehood that the king had been gruesomely murdered by the war maniacs of the barbaric enemy forces. "Despite my desperate attempt to give him legitimate salvation, to save his royal life by losing mine," he is reported to have added with sympathetic tears. And whom do you think the kingdom would have chosen as the assassinated King's most deserving successor? The standard bearer of course, both assassin and legitimate saviour!

"Those are the complexities of the world!", my talkative grandfather was used to saying, whenever I came rushing to tell him that our neighbour's son had beaten me.

And how right he was! To succeed to the throne of a king, one needs inordinate ambition, a dead conscience, an assassin, a God-sent opportunity, a lie and a malleable people. And once this end has been attained, one must never, never forget to wipe off the earth's face all those who directly helped one up one's ambitious ladder. Failure to do just that makes one even more vulnerable than one's predecessor. (The very same standard bearer in our story had helped his victim succeed to the throne by defeating the army of a certain Duke of Milan, who had also wanted to become king. That had happened long ago, before he became too ambitious to be contented with being 'just' a standard bearer.) That explains why most of those who have tried to be conciliatory after an illegitimate or controversial accession to power have met with catastrophic fates. For as Manu Dibango, Cameroon's most celebrated musician so aptly sings, "L'Ennemi ne dort jamais, jamais, jamais"; the enemy is always awake, always alert.

The second case in point is the most recent of them all. The episode took place in a country where superstition is ten times more advanced than science. It is perhaps from the Englishman's fantastic experiences in this country of the world that he came about the saying: "Life is larger than Logic". And I must add that when a white man openly admits something about the Dark Zones of the world, when he suddenly finds reason to consult his stars before taking a major decision, even to the detriment of his hullabaloo about science and Cartesian rationalism, when this happens, know that that 'Something' is a tremendous force to reckon with.

The leader of this country was not a king; he was an elected President. He had judged his popularity from the votes he was alleged to have had at the election where he happened to be the only candidate: 100 per cent. This meant that he was supposedly popular with every single person of voting age in his country. And because those not yet of the age to vote are almost always led like sheep, we can venture to say that he was 100 per cent popular with voters and non voters alike. Yet he was killed! And not even his bodyguards amongst whom he was reportedly most popular did a thing to save him! Whence was this political enemy who transformed himself into a green serpent to bite him to death, while his bodyguards fired shots of encouragement instead? Was he not part of the 100 per cent popularity? Doesn't a 100 per cent mean that one has the absolute confidence of one's people, and that one doesn't really need to go about with bodyguards amongst people who love one so fully?

But our President was as unfortunate as his Third World country; surely he suffered from paranoia. If not, how can a world leader of normal intelligence ever imagine such elusive a thing as 100 per cent popularity? Even a tyrant would take that with a pinch of salt. If Lucifer did oppose God, it indicates that absolute support is as much a celestial impossibility as it is terrestrial. So if he died from Heaven to Hell, he did so to serve the cause of human knowledge. He was sacrificed on the altar of knowledge so that world leaders might learn from his mistakes by relinquishing the vice of ignorance. Woe betides those leaders who still believe in the anachronism of total and unconditional support in this era of widespread democracy!

Some Third World leaders would honestly argue that their electorates freely choose to give them 100 per cent support. How naive! One such leader from Africa went to the UN to sell the idea that his country was a shining example of democracy. As head of the sole ruling party he had just been returned to power with a 99.99 per cent. He even declared at the UN that had his wife not died suddenly before the elections, he would have had a glaring 100 per cent. Her death had taken off .01 per cent of his total.

Probably encouraged by his convincing tone, the UN voted that an upcoming conference on "Instability in Third World governments" be held in his country. He was flattered and went ahead with all the necessary preparations. At last, the conference took place and was well attended. But barely three days after the conference, our 99.99 per cent popular President was assassinated in a bloody coup d'état. One of his army generals had attended the conference and followed with keen interest a scholarly paper on "How to conduct a successful coup d'état". Had our president been slightly more modest, he might have lived.

This particular story reminds me of an African President who is totally realistic. And I dare say it is better to be over than under in one's realism. Though he came to power through a coup d'état himself, he is very severe on all those who would wish he left it by the same means. When an attempt is made to force him out through the same backdoor through which he sneaked in, he becomes most obsessed with the principles of raw democracy and unfettered justice. His idea of justice is guided by jungle law and democracy makes sense only when it fosters his perverse quest for sadistic vengeance. Subversion is redefined to mean anything likely to undermine the president's authority, illegitimate though the latter may be. Many would say he is inhuman, brutal and barbaric. But I would preferably stress another aspect: His realism. He knows he came to power because he loved power, not because he wanted to contribute towards solving the plethoric problems of underdevelopment that face his country. He makes no secret of the fact that he is as useful to his people as a hungry hawk is to a group of day-old chicks.

With his aim so eloquently defined, why should he come short of using every available means towards its attainment? Perhaps he is very pleased to have realised his childhood dream to become thrice richer than his country. Then he surely, when in good humour of course, would negotiate financial aid with his country at exorbitant interest rates. Yet what preoccupies me is not so much his kindness, as the ridiculous idea that an individual can be richer than his own country. Whence come his riches? God alone knows. What an admirable man! He is at least less hypocritical than some of his counterparts elsewhere who overtly accuse him of butchery and opposition phobia, but who would stop at nothing to conceal their own records of flagrant butchery, human rights violations and economic cannibalism.

Power is a wonderful commodity. The human community attaches more value to it than it does to Gold. Nobody ever seems to have enough of it, not even those who have been exposed to it most. Instead, the more one is used to power, the more one craves it. Strange thing, power is, so capable of making tyrants of even the most well-intentioned democratic or chicken-minded of individuals. All and sundry pay regular consultation visits at the Temple of Power. Young ambitions go there to ask: "Whose turn is it next?", while old ambitions ask for "Just another chance to put right past wrongs". But unlike many other cults, power appeals to both the master and the servant, the dominator and the dominated. For the former is fearful of his fate if favour should but fail to smile on him, and the latter is so desirous of seeing what is inside that Holy Shrine of Power that whichever priest ventures in is suddenly obsessed with the idea of priesthood for life!

Thoughts of power make me most sad. I try to avoid them as much as I can, but I keep having them willy-nilly. They are like an all-consuming conflagration. These thoughts make me ask, bitterly, why so many leaders are so self-centred that they throw to the winds the legitimate aspirations of their people. Why do leaders not realise that there is something morally abhorrent about an individual who strives to place himself above his society? Who deceives them into thinking that a man can be greater than the society whence he springs? Can a child be so hard hearted as to turn around and spit on the womb that carried it about for nine months? That, I think, is the height of mean arrogance and base beastliness!

To close this chapter on power, there is last month's issue of the *African Dream* magazine which was banned from circulation in this country. But this latest ban wasn't any more successful than previous ones. A few hundred copies went underground and continued to change hands astonishingly quickly. I came across a stray copy in one of the seats of 'The Giant Millipede' and took immediate advantage of it. A more chicken-hearted Cameroonian had probably dropped it on recognising a plainclothes policeman. Inside the magazine was a daring article written in the form of a letter from an African in Europe to his friend in Africa. One paragraph touched me in a powerful way.

"Moungo," the author writes, "Tell me in earnest, if you were a leader and happened to be overthrown in a bloodless coup d'état, would you carry all the country's money away with you in a Land Rover? Or would you, faced with severe economic crisis, believe that the simple way out is just to print more bank notes and flood the country with them? Would you think that the best way of impressing your foreign counterparts and friends is by giving them the only precious stones that can earn your country some foreign reserve? Would you preach African Socialism, yet find nothing wrong with purchasing a £40,000 bed for your concubine? Would you proceed to celebrate the tenth anniversary of the revolution that brought you to power, when the rural people were threatened by the very famine and malnourishment which greased the way to your revolution a decade ago? Would you deprive an innocent people of the roads, water and electricity that they badly need, just because you consider a member of their tribe to be a political thorn in your flesh? Would you consider yourself as a superman who knows all, and therefore should not be advised? Would you believe yourself when you try to make others believe that there is only one route to progress, and that route is you? Would you arise one fine morning and order the massive extermination of every child whose parents are too poor to purchase for them school uniforms that bear your effigy? Would you stop every other woman from bearing the name Monique, just because it happens to be your wife's? And would you sneak in through the back door to seize the power which you held for twenty years and more, but which you freely gave up because your Western doctors mistakenly advised you that a long time in power was bad for your health? Whether you accept what I say or not, bear in mind that many an African leader has done more outrageous things."

What a letter! What oratory! Delivered as a political speech anywhere in Africa, this paragraph would incite the populace to rise and protest their oppression. Biting to those in power though the whole letter seems to be, it hurts nobody in particular. No one is singled out for castigation. Nowhere in it is special reference made to Cameroon. I would have thought that its very general and anecdotal nature would shield it from the harsh axe of the administrative censor. If governments can be so obsessive as to ban things written in such general terms, what hope is there that their peoples would ever come to read about the things that touch them most?

Lord God, forgive me for allowing myself to be carried away by thoughts that are by no means connected with this religion. Help orient my thoughts to a more fertile terrain of concern. Grant me the ability to distinguish between the trivial and the weighty. Enhance my power to understand your Holy Word. I ask thee through Jesus

Christ my saviour, whom I invite to come and dwell in me throughout the rest of this day. Amen.

Yes, I feel better now. How great the power of prayer must be! I was already overflowing with guilt. Sometimes I find myself agreeing with those who affirm that religion should be a man's personal affair with his God, not a congregational affair. I mean those who would argue that the Church, being a human institution, is run by people who are not less fallible than we the ordinary Christians, and therefore ought to claim no moral superiority whatsoever. The Pope and his team of clergymen are like everyone else – just struggling to be good, and often, they are not as successful in their struggles as the average layman. Imagine how two minutes of absolute concentration in prayer has brought me almost face to face with God. What clergyman would lay claims to a quicker response than I just had? Within a couple of minutes I've felt God's love and peace coil into me like a holy serpent, enriching and pacifying my beleaguered heart and mind.

However, there is a limit to how long one can concentrate. And whoever alleges that a man can concentrate throughout a two-hour mass ridden with boring paraphrases and senseless recitations must be joking! Let the clergy research into how best the mass can be delivered!

Meanwhile the mass continues to the end without the Honourable V.M. The atmosphere in the church is actually different without him. The change is visible all over. Somehow I feel relieved of his presence, power and authority. Could the others be feeling the same? I can't say, but the Honourable V.M certainly has a most pervasive presence in church. The mass seems to lose its meaning, especially now that Rev. Father Limbo has started to rush it in the absence of the Honourable V.M. Perhaps the priest doesn't want to be late for an after-service appointment. Priests aren't exactly entirely for the church, are they? The rest of the congregation doesn't seem to want to stay a minute longer either. That, I can understand, as neither Dr T, Mrs S, nor Prof. N is in church today. I wonder why they are absent, all three of them. Maybe they chose to go to the Cathedral instead; their French is good after all. Anyway, without any of these persons, with the Honourable V.M gone, and with a priest who is racing against time, what is the mass worth again? What else can I say but intercede the Almighty on behalf of the lowly of heart and status? Lord God, heavenly Father, kindly restore to the mass the glimmer it presently lacks. May we witness a brighter mass Sunday next.

PART TWO

This Sunday is a special one here in Nsam. Ten new converts are to be baptised. But that isn't what gives the day a particular note. Rather, what makes everyone alert is that among the would-be Christians are the children of the Honourable V.M, Dr T, Mrs S, and Prof. N. No one ignores what this means. Preparations have been going on for the past week in the various residences towards the celebrations of this special initiation ceremony. The congregation is reminded of the festivities that such well-to-do families have always had in store at any major occasion. So they are all expectant, and rightly so.

How carefully designed certain things seem! Why have the children of the Honourable V.M, Dr T, Mrs S, and Prof. N waited to be baptised at the same time, all nine of them? Everyone knows that the parents negotiated with the priest. It is true that all four families are very close to Rev. Father Limbo, but still.... Mrs S for instance is known to invite him over to her place for meals twice a week. Who doesn't know that in order to fuel his car the priest uses petrol coupons ("les bonds d'essence") generously donated by the Honourable V.M, and dearly paid for by the state? Hasn't Dr T's name gone down in the "Church Book of Records" as the most generous contributor towards the purchase of the parish car which Rev. Father Limbo inherited from Le Père Jean Mouton? As for Prof. N, it is simply his great learnedness that accounts for his fame and that of his family. His book: The History of Christianity in the Western Grassfields has been decreed a bestseller by the Vatican. He writes songs for the church and sometimes advocates the teaching of Religious Knowledge to school children. But he is said to be controversial in his refusal to have the Bible translated into Pidgin English, the language of the majority of Christians. "The Holy Book must not be desecrated," he says, meaning that the Bible's 'original' language, which also happens to be the language of Shakespeare his literary idol, must not be tampered with. I strongly feel that he would be the first to receive Holy Communion from the papal chalice, if the Pope should ever decide to ramble into Cameroon. While the Honourable V.M and a handful of others could politically follow in any order after the deserving reward of this servant of God's. It's a pity that his Holiness the Pope would tire himself to death if he decided to be generous with my countrymen; for he is going to have an incredibly long queue of important faithfuls all wishing to communicate with God through him! Apart from that, I would personally advise him to enlist the services of a seasoned diviner who would be able to differentiate between the Christians and the Moslems in this country where political ambition can push people to commit all sorts of religious fallacies.

All dressed in sparkling white, the converts are comparable to angels. The ceremony is normally long and tiring, but the priest is particularly fast and interesting. Perhaps he knows what is at stake here. Today's seems to be the only sermon without paraphrases; it is an apt commentary on the symbolic significance of baptism. He says for instance that "initiation into Christianity is just like becoming an important member of the Unified Party." I may be accused of over inquisitiveness, but I would like to know why Rev. Father Limbo should endanger his priestly competence by meddling with politics? He must have a very short memory, this priest! Has he already forgotten the "Nkoulou affair", where a bishop was audacious enough to provide sanctuary to "a terrorist leader", and almost lost his life? He certainly wouldn't say he no longer remembers when the President, like a wounded lion, asked to be brought Bishop Nkoulou's head on a silver platter? He must be careful what he says. May he be taken in good faith!

Everyone listens to him preach. I wish he would preach like this ever after. It shows he is capable of much more than mere paraphrases.... Certainly not! These trouble-makers and rumour-mongers can never be absent. They always have a derogatory remark to make. Hear the mean things they whisper. "Stop that! Stop being so mean you devils!" I wish I could hush them down. But I just can't, so they whisper on. Hear the way they say it! You would believe every word of it, if you didn't know better! How can they be so anti-Christian as to think that Rev. Father Limbo is preaching so diligently because he expects remuneration from the wealthy parents of his new converts? I wonder how much money they paid the priest when they were being baptised themselves? Perhaps they might retort by saying, "When we were baptised, the clergy wasn't as materialistic as it is today." And am I to believe that our priest would like to be seen as part of a materialistic clergy? No, not I! I only believe what is expected of a good Roman Catholic Christian. The Rev. Father Limbo is jolly well doing his duty as the competent tool of God he knows that he is. That's what I believe, no more no less.

The church is full to capacity. I am again unlucky, having to stand throughout this unusually long service. The Honourable

V.M's bodyguards are sleeping in his black Mercedes 280 SE parked outside the church. Yes, this time the thugs are actually sleeping, not simply snoring with their eyes wide open. Strange enough, this sudden change in routine, isn't it? On second thoughts, I reckon I am wicked by failing to understand them; and by so doing, I'm no better than the Honourable V.M who makes them work round the clock as if they were robots. Aren't they human, built of the same substance as the man for whom they sacrifice rest, sleep and life?

The actual baptism has started. The priest begins the ritual by reading out passages from an assorted number of books, some of which are in Latin, but most of which are in English. The sermon was good, quite interesting; but these readings are nothing but an anticlimax. The lengthy passages bore one to death; they always have. Can't these priests understand that something is wrong with their system and approach, and that they ought to start thinking of how to make their teachings both relevant and captivating? Why cannot Rev. Father Limbo, for example, test those converts kneeling in front of him at the moment to see if they understand all the junk he has been reciting nonstop? I think he might have learnt from last Sunday's episode, when he said: "There is something wrong with this microphone," and the congregation retorted: "And also with you". He should have known thence that when the mass is boring, the congregation is absent-minded. The present congregation is even more so, now that festivities are to follow after this ritual. Some of the people are already dozing off when the real ceremony has barely commenced. I must say I'm tired myself. This standing isn't an easy thing to do, particularly for someone who hasn't eaten. My legs are hurting like mad. Strange, the resistance the human mechanism can put up!

Why is the church so full when this baptism ceremony was not announced beforehand? Of course it's intuition! When there is beer and champagne after mass, men even become more intuitive than their wives. That is why looking at the congregation, one remarks that for the first time ever, the men have almost outnumbered the women. Usually, the left-hand side of the church is more populated than the right. Perhaps the various families involved in today's baptismal ceremony did send out invitations to their relations and acquaintances. But if that is the case, I'm surprised that the Honourable V.M. didn't send me an invitation. I should think myself his friend, shouldn't I? It isn't to every Tom, Dick and Harry that one gives a gift, is it?

I might just be mistaken in blaming the Honourable V.M for failing to remember me as a friend. Suppose, just suppose he did remember me, and did actually want to send me an invitation card, how would he have gone about it? How would he have traced me? Driven himself through every narrow street of Briqueterie, stopping by every falling hut to ask for "My friend Judascious Fanda Yanda"? Or sticked around Le Cinema du Pays hoping to see me come out, tired from watching a violent Hong Kong Kung Fu movie? Just how did I expect my friend, if friend he is, to get in touch with me between two Sundays? For I must not forget that although the Honourable V.M and I are known to live in the same great city, our worlds are totally different from one another's. Bastos has virtually nothing in common with Briqueterie. Even their physical locations emphasise their differences. Bastos is located on a hill at the foot of which is Briqueterie. Seen in terms of Jacob's Ladder, Bastos would be on the topmost rung far up in the skies and close to Heaven, proudly looking down on Briqueterie still on the ground, struggling to have its feet on the first rung. Historically, both residential areas were first settled by people from opposite strata of society. Bastos' very first settler was a white administrator. Employed by him was a group of black masons who, respectful of their master, chose to live below the hill. They named their village Briqueterie, meaning, the place where bricks are manufactured. Surrounding Briqueterie are Mokolo, Tsinga, Grand Messa, the commercial centre and Nlongkak. None of these residential areas are as miserable as Briqueterie; they are not as well off as Bastos either.

In Bastos, houses are constructed in lines. The streets are broad and straight. They are named, although none of these names is familiar, because they are all French. At the end of each street is a letter box. The houses are numbered, which makes it easy for the mailman to deliver letters right to the door. Briqueterie on the other hand is totally different. It is a misnomer to call what one finds there 'houses'. These are huts which all look as though they would fall apart at one moment or another. The streets are narrow, very narrow indeed. They are also muddy, because to say the truth, they are not streets in the real sense of the word. They happen to be footpaths which have gradually broadened up through the years. Everything in Briqueterie is muddled up. It is a place where A's backyard is B's front yard, and I must say this causes many problems. Take the issue of bathroom and latrines for example. You really need to go to certain parts of

Briqueterie to know the way they smell. Imagine yourself eating with friends in your little hut, and imagine your neighbour answering nature's call in a latrine just in front of your hut. You actually see him do it, but you can't ask him to stop because he is in his backyard. And by the way, if he were to listen to you and stop doing it, where else does he go to answer nature's call? Thus with such basic hygienic problems unresolved, how would we expect Briqueterie to have letter boxes on every street?

Oh! Yes! It is now I understand that my mind might make things appear so different from what they really are. Wasn't it silly of me to expect the impossible from the Honourable V.M? I stay right in the muddy heart of Briqueterie, where there is neither house nor light, but where all is a bustling ghetto that booms with resistant life, defying the threatening cords of overdue death. How can one thus situated imagine such fantastic an illusion as an address? The Honourable V.M might be quite well intentioned, but how does he translate this to his nameless faceless friend, if friend I am?

Is this the price one must pay for an ensuing feast? I mean having to go through the entire ritual, boring as it is. I would like just to leave the church, and to forget about everything. But can I, am I prepared to miss the feast? I know that my presence at the celebrations is forfeited, once I dare leave the church or turn my back to the children of Dr T, Mrs S, Prof. N and the Honourable V.M. Why can't the wealthy of the society treat the poor with some respect? Why all these indirections? To eat and drink with a dignitary one must attend a long and boring baptism ceremony, and must pretend to be interested by it. For it won't be strange if someone is busy taking down the names of those who at this very moment are sleeping instead of actively participating in the ritual. So that nobody should express surprise if his ration is curtailed, or if he isn't invited to partake in the festivities at the end of the baptism ceremony.

I will do my best to stay awake and alert. I don't want to disappoint my friend the Honourable V.M. It would be very bad indeed for me if he learns that I slept during his daughter's baptism. Thus to keep myself active and to stay awake, I will indulge in an alternative mind-searching exercise. So far I've searched only my own mind, but what a pleasurable pastime will it be to turn my attention towards others and their thoughts! And, I decide to guess what can possibly be going on in the mind of some members of the congregation picked at random, just by reading their countenances. I hope this little exercise is recreational enough to chase boredom away without also chasing away my would-be hosts, for I really look forward to the festivities after the baptism!

Were I to put my thoughts down on paper just the way they have occurred to me so far, and were I to attempt to have them published, I'm pretty sure they might make no sense to readers who are used to having stories presented in an orderly way with clearly defined themes, sophisticated plots, and consistent styles. But I'm sure that among my readers as well would be some who know that writers are always trying to force order into their chaotic mental processes, and to pretend their thoughts are always consistent, disciplined and profound. But to be honest with ourselves, is that really the way our thoughts normally appear to us? Have we ever stopped for a while to ask ourselves why we sometimes write, cancel, and rewrite? Does that say anything about how much time we spend trying to trim and prune our thoughts into shape? Were we to present every single thought of ours, in exactly the same way that they occur to us, are we sure that our presentation would be as orderly, consistent, and disciplined, as we tend to make believe? If ever I decide to become a writer, I would have to write the way I think, even if this means writing only for myself, as would most likely be the case. My point made, à nos moutons once again.

Many members of this congregation may be physically bored, but mentally they are not. Their bodies are imprisoned by the ceremony, but their minds are free to go on the most fantastic of trips. Society might place certain physical and verifiable limitations on its members, it might equally do so mentally by injecting a moral code of conduct into their minds; but the fundamental freedom is that a man's thoughts can always go unsanctioned if he declines to make them manifest. So I see many people having recourse to this mental advantage. No one wants to be completely shackled. There is much to be gained even in the illusion of freedom. Could I guess that in a highly repressive society, people think a lot, because thoughts happen to be the only safe way by which they can vent their frustrations and dissatisfaction with the authorities in place?

There is this young lady on my right. I met her standing where she is at the moment. It is doubtless that she is undergoing some serious mental torture, from the way she sweats, her clouded forehead and her apparent absent-mindedness. In addition, she is constantly sighing and cursing. I can hear her snap her fingers every now and again. Whenever I steal a look at her, I catch her in the act of contemplating her painted long fingernails. With such nails, she can be worse than a tiger to any male who tries to take advantage of her! I'm told women don't grow nails simply for the beauty of it. I can tell, just by looking that this young lady is most upset. Poor thing! What could be the matter with her?

On her T-shirt is the inscription "Look At My Shoes". I do just that and notice that they are worth a Sunday pair. For the shoes are expensive looking, rare and delicate, just what every woman would sacrifice a treasure to acquire. Many men would love to find another inscription altogether: Perhaps "Look At My Skirt" or "My Legs", etc., for their own idiosyncratic reasons. Somehow the men would think that an invitation to look at such an expensive pair of shoes is in fact an implicit invitation to see what she is worth as a girl.

Unfortunately, the saying that nothing can be all gold holds true for her. I do feel profoundly sorry for this beautiful girl whose pair of shoes gives her physical discomfort and even aggravates or generates mental malaise. Perhaps she regrets having spent so much money to purchase just the wrong size of shoes. Maybe she was deceived by a dishonest man to indebt herself to Miss E who imports dresses, footwear, oils and cosmetics from Europe for sale to high-class women. Or maybe she insisted on having the only pair flown over from Italy for exhibition here in the great city, mainly because she would love to go on record as the first girl ever to put on that particular design of shoes in the country. It adds points to one's social significance, you know? This girl wouldn't suffer her present discomfort without complaint, if there was nothing to it.

The girl in question might be a student at the National University, and as such her problems should be many. Perhaps she used all of this month's scholarship to purchase her shoes and is consequently compelled to bland meals of bread and water. Perhaps she doesn't have the scholarship and has to depend on rich parents or on the dubious generosity of male friends. Her problems might be much more complex than I have imagined. Maybe she has agreed to be housed by a young man who is incapable of assuring their meals and rents, one who is so poor, yet so loving. She might simply be a very realistic girl who is befriending one of those young, dynamic and able cooks at the University Restaurant, who provides her with the food she needs in exchange for sexual pleasures and whom her friends disapprove of by saying "common little thing", behind her back.

On the other hand, she might be a very self-satisfied lady with no financial problems at all. She might hate to look cheap in front of men. In which case her problem might be an academic one, if it still holds that she is a student in the National University. For, there, hearsay holds it that lecturers are poor financially, but rich academically. They tell girls that the golden key to success lies beneath their skirts. But to their male students they say something entirely different: That the rusty key to failure lies in their heads and perhaps, in their unwary attempt to eat with their academic elders at the same table.

Yes, I can testify to this, thanks to hearsay. They are real lechers, those lecturers. How many times have I overheard a group of enraged male students? Countless. And what do they always complain of? Lecturers, lecherous lecturers, who invade the homes of their girlfriends, get caught in compromising positions, are humiliated and then chased home in shame and nakedness. But the very next day, they conspire with the police, and have the male students arrested and detained. What a vicious cycle! And what a school of scandal!

But whatever the case, whatever problems preoccupy this girl on my right are entirely her affair. I must be honest with myself that there is little I can do to help her. If only she knew that I stay at Briqueterie under most deplorable conditions, and that I barely have enough to eat, she would immediately abandon her worries and offer a special prayer of thanks to God, or perhaps simply participate fully in the mass in order to clear her conscience for the feast to follow. She must remember that no pleasure comes without sacrifice. She can't cheat by going to eat and drink at the expense of Dr T, Mrs S, Prof. N, and the Honourable V.M, if she has helped in no way towards getting their children closer to Heaven.

There is a girl next to me on the left. But I don't want to speculate about her. Her behaviour is extremely unsympathetic. She is wearing a straw hat and a veil that hides her beauty, or that makes me think she might be ugly. And when I turn towards her, or repeat a prayer looking in her direction, she winces at my smell. It is true that I didn't brush my mouth this morning, because my toothpaste finished yesterday, and it is true that I haven't had a wash for days, because there is something wrong with the communal taps that supply water in Briqueterie; but isn't it too arrogant of her to show such detestation of a fellow church member like myself? And wouldn't it be justifiable if I hated her for that? But I won't; my mind is too clean to hate, isn't it?

Sitting directly behind the Honourable V.M is a young man in a dark brown suit. His hair is fashionably curly, and I dare say he must have spent a fortune to have it done for him. He is as good looking as Dr T, but far younger. He might also be more fruitful than the latter who, it is rumoured, invites his brother to make his children for him in order to evade the ignominy that comes with barrenness. I can't read his countenance because I am standing far away from his seat. However, I feel worried that he should sit where he sits. He appears like a tiger poised to attack the Honourable V.M at the slightest opportunity. He could also be compared to a hawk perching on a tree, waiting for the right moment to snatch the ministry that the Honourable V.M guards with the watchfulness of a mother hen.

Perhaps he is a politically ambitious lad who somehow feels that the Honourable V.M does not deserve his place. Maybe he is one of these learned men who wrongly believe that Western education is a prerequisite to good leadership. I would rather they believe that Western education is the best means to become an academic simpleton, and a contextual misfit. Those who advocate the former thesis have a lot to learn from precolonial leadership in many parts of this country. There is the brilliant example of a bald-headed clown who, after reading all the books he could find in England, returned to his tribe to ask the chief to abdicate in favour of civilised leadership. But fortunately for him, he was picked up and imprisoned for subversion by the central authorities, long before his tribe and ancestors had decided on how best to sanction him for his unfounded arrogance and suicidal disrespect. It is said that during the era of multiparty politics, a potential candidate lost the singular opportunity of becoming Prime Minister because he forgot that no man, no matter how important, is allowed the privilege of shaking hands with a Grassfields king.

So I would like the Honourable V.M to be very alert. That young man looks dangerous and ought to be watched at close range. I don't know the tribe from which the Honourable V.M comes. But I do know that if he is unwary, even the policy of regional planning would be unable to save him if the young man should strike. It is true that things are far from straight in this triangle of ours, but it is very important to know what motivates this young man. Granted my guess on his political ambition to be true, is his zeal to replace the Honourable V.M motivated by selfish considerations, or by the desire to contribute to the public good? Public good as defined by whom? And from whose point of view? Isn't it true that the hunter's dog does not always place its spoils in front of its master? Or that usually it doesn't even think of the master, when it immediately starts to eat the game it has stalked, leaving the said master to show how much he needs the catch by fighting to seize it? Nothing is more difficult to determine just by reading countenances or by speculating on people's intentions.

The young man looks too sophisticated to be an uncontaminated country fellow of mine. His dressing and apparent self-consecrated importance are quite incompatible with our "manière de faire". There are precisely such young men who strive for 'radical' changes in the society, radical, yet not recognisable by the people the very same changes are meant to please. They think that what took decades to construct can be eradicated in a day, and replaced with a poor Western equivalent which they brought back in the pocket of their winter coat. Their impatience with their fathers' ways and traditions is indicative of their marked inexperience. The fault is in the itinerary of their student life, and the content of their education. Their ideas of our country are forged in Europe and then flown in, hot and ready to be put into practice. How do you expect youngsters who have spent all their childhood with whites, reading about whites, not to think and act like whites? How do we expect a plant grown in a test tube to be as firm as one with roots in the soil? How do we expect an imported chicken grown in a record time of two weeks, to taste the same as our local chicken that takes seven years to mature? How do we expect a blind man to see simply because he has a pair of eyes just like everyone else around him?

There are many real examples of such made in Europe young men. They brandish their academic qualifications everywhere they go, aspiring to replace their 'half-witted elders', thinking that their pieces of paper would perform miracles. They are very impatient with men like the Honourable V.M, who has the uncanny ability to read party handouts upside down, and to sign their own political death warrants without being aware, endorsing every single scheme designed by their party leader, who loves power like a vampire does blood. This young man might know next to nothing about the country he plans to take over. All he is obsessed about is the actual takeover. He can't even say why his country is known as 'Africa in Miniature', because he has spent precious time reading only about fourth and fifth republics in the

West. Suppose I told him that Cameroon is 'Africa In Miniature' because it embodies every single vice that one is likely to identify in other African countries. He might say "Yes, you are correct. That's exactly why". To hell with him, won't you say? Worst of all, this young man might not even be bilingual.

And what leader does he intend to make in a country with many linguistic cleavages? Continue with the same old tradition of one linguistic group addressing the other from the room above, and not caring if they are understood or not? And would that, according to him, be developing the nation? Once more I say to hell with him and his ambition! But he might not be that ambitious after all. I'm simply speculating, am I not?

The baptism is now over. Thank God for it. The children are now Christians. They have agreed to reject "Satan and all his ways". Christ has gained access into their hearts and has become their guiding spirit, their torch through the darkness of this continent. But in some time to come, these new Christians are going to have their faith put to the test, just as happened to the rest of us. They are also going to be bothered by the new breed of Christians who Rev. Father Limbo and other clerics have described as locusts, and whom they have denounced without compunction. Several weeks ago

Rev. Father Limbo asked us to beware, not to fall prey to "these 'Born Agains' who claim to be closer to Christ than even the heavenly dignitaries, who say they actually know our Saviour more than the Maries ever did!" I wonder why they have been nicknamed 'The Born Agains'? Or have they chosen to call themselves that? I also wonder why Rev. Father Limbo has not talked to his new converts about these 'Born Agains'? Doesn't he think his young Christians ought to be well prepared for their battles against Satan and all his ways, right from the beginning?

Yes, I believe he is wrong not to speak to them about Satan. His silence on the issue shows complacency. But for Heaven's sake, why should he be complacent? He must not lead me into thinking that I'm alone in seeing what is there for him to see as well! I notice so many things which other members of this congregation do that contradict what they profess to believe. Perhaps I see the things I see because I live in Briqueterie, which is like sinful bait, tempting the Christians to come along and indulge in base pleasure. But the priest should even know better since these Christians eventually confess all their sins to him. Right here in this very ugly triangle are some twenty or so people I have personally caught red handed, committing sin. There is a vulgar nightclub in Briqueterie so famous for its cheap women that it has been nicknamed 'The Market for Women' ('La Marché de Femmes'). Each night one finds as many women in the 'market' as maggots in a rotting carcass. It is there that men go to pick up women. On Saturdays at night, you can find men from all walks of life, groping into Briqueterie to fish for women, and groping out again. But whatever they do, however much they drink or oversleep, they are always in time for Sunday mass, which is like a clearance to their hangovers.

One must never find it strange that things should change. The clergy must know and learn to accept the fact that as Christians experience changing economic circumstances, the church's doctrines are not always going to be relevant. I remember the laughter Rev. Father Limbo incited when he criticised the modern tendency in couples to consider themselves truly married once a mayor has given them a civil status certificate. When he deplored this attitude, and went out of his way to say that it was wrong for any couple thus married to communicate with Christ, the congregation merely burst into jeers. I believe they found his point of view on this issue very outmoded. After all, they know that the financial expenses involved in a church wedding have reached such an astronomical height that there is every reason to abandon aspirations for such a singular honour. Moreover the civil authorities have offered a more attractive alternative. Just in a matter of seconds a mayor's signature does the trick and binds the couple, saving months of impatience and boredom going through tedious ecclesiastical formalities. It is also the better alternative for the struggling young and poor. Just think how long it would take a young employee, toiling to sustain body and soul in an urban centre like this, to muster enough funds to permit him to wed at God's altar. A Church wedding and its advocates are rapidly becoming outmoded, and soon marriage will be just civil or traditional.

This issue of marriage brings to mind a story I had almost forgotten. It is about one of the leading kings in the Grassfields of the country. This particular king had a son whom he sent as far abroad as England to train. His son returned home after obtaining his Doctorate in History or "Doctor of Book" as he rapidly came to be known locally. The whole kingdom was disappointed with a doctor who instead of curing the sick in his community could only attend to sick books. The king, who alone seemed to understand what on earth his son had spent huge sums of money trying to learn abroad, felt that this son of his should marry in the traditional way of his people, since he was his most likely successor.

But nobody goes to Europe and comes back to listen to anyone, not even a father who also happens to be king. So the king's son normally had his own Western ideas to put forth, and a good backing for them as well. According to the prince that he was, it was imperative that he should get married following he modern precepts prescribed by the white man's church. He considered his decision a necessary one because it could both uphold the respectable image of leadership his father held among the kings of the region, and reconcile him with the radical moderns who felt there was nothing worth retaining in the past ways of thinking and doing. The king yielded to his son's plausible argument, after making him promise that he would at least be smeared with camwood and palm oil a week or so after the church wedding.

The marriage was scheduled to take place in the biggest church in the parish. The rich king was ready to sponsor it. So his son could afford to think of making it the most extravagant wedding ever conducted in the parish. The parishioners looked forward to the event with joy, happy to be involved in the wedding of a prince. News spread far and wide that the king was to attend mass for the first time ever. So on the day of the wedding the church was full with Christians and pagans, who had come to see what mass looked like with a king in church. The white priest, a certain Rev. Father Isaac Blackhead was slow at coming out of the sacristy. Meanwhile the king had asked for his stool to be placed in the front of the church, closest to the altar, so he would be able to register every single detail of the ceremony. He wanted to see his son and daughter-in-law, and be satisfied with himself. There he sat, quite detached from the congregation, but waiting with them for the tardy priest.

When the priest at last turned up he stopped abruptly, immobilized by fury. On seeing the king sitting quite apart from the others and wearing a traditional cap on which was inserted a black feather, he felt his church and God belittled. So he charged towards the king who was quite unperturbed. The congregation watched with keenness and anxiety. And he did what they had all feared. He slapped the king across the face and pulled off the cap – symbol of the king's office and traditional authority. But the king merely laughed, stood up and walked out of the church, his retainers behind him with his stool and paraphernalia. The rest of the story was narrated to him later on: How just when the priest was about to begin saying the mass, a strange lightning from nowhere struck him dead. And so the priest lost his life and perhaps the only opportunity to strike a compromise between Christianity and the Grassfields tradition. Today the feud between the church and traditional values brings nothing but bitter memories to each camp. But one question remains unanswered, and perhaps always will be. Would our unfortunate priest have asked the Archbishop or the Pope for that matter, to take up their own caps? Perhaps the answer is clear and straightforward, and I'm simply too stupid to see it.

The mass has just ended. Rev. Father Limbo has given his final blessings. Rev. Sister B. has also finished making the after-mass announcements. Now all eyes are turned on Dr T, the spokesman for the parents of the converts. He mounts the podium. The ugly triangle is silent with expectancy. He takes his time to cough and fidget with his papers, and to readjust his necktie. It is very hot in here, I can understand why he sweats so profusely. What a bad day for those in suits! Dr T knows how to capture a crowd's attention; he has a magic personality. Others would say that he has salt on his tongue. Most public figures in this capital city are good at capturing crowds. A neighbouring President once declared at a news conference that he was a man of action not a man of words. "If you want beautiful speeches and bewitching orators," he told the group of journalists who were questioning him, "you should go across the border to Cameroon where even two-year olds can harangue a crowd." He implied that here speech-making is as much an institution as any other.

At last Dr T makes the long awaited speech. He certainly isn't at his best; his voice is plain and unexciting. What is the matter with him? Perhaps the heat is responsible. Yes, the heat, it must be the heat. Still fidgeting with his tie and the buttons of his suit, he says what everyone has waited to hear. The whole congregation is invited to the residence of the Honourable V.M for the collective celebration of the baptism of their children. Just to show what good people they are, he explains to the congregation how the Honourable V.M, Prof. N, Mrs S and himself have decided to ask the only other person baptised together with their children, to come along and be their child too. The congregation laughs because he is talking about a forty year old Briqueterie woman. But everyone appreciates their generous offer to a convert who is too poor to throw her own party. The church fervently applauds as he promises free transportation for everyone to and from the Honourable V.M's residence. So all we need do is assemble ourselves outside the church and wait to be carried to Bastos in special buses. I feel as if I am about to undertake a trip to Heaven.

☆ ☆ ☆

This bus is good indeed, superbly comfortable, although most of the roads are appalling. It is quite unlike the overcrowded AVOC buses where services are dished out most grudgingly as if the company were being forced to make money against their will. I hate to think that those poorly brought up, loosely coordinated drivers and ticket controllers defied their inefficient services and poor conditions to swindle me. May they meet with greater success in this daily means of livelihood... And may they continue to chase after the widow's mite instead of making real money.

I wish I could take a ride round the city like this all year long. That would keep me abreast with the recent developments in the city, for it is by going out and seeing for oneself that one avoids being easily deceived by second hand accounts. I would no longer content myself with the newspaper version of things, nor with what is filtered through the airwaves. I may better understand why more and more of my fellow countrymen tend to think that suicide is the best solution to the castigating frustrations of their daily lives. I might also come to understand why the outside world always appears to be more versed with our national realities than we the nationals are. For example, why is it we never know when the President has left the country for a private visit to Europe, and are only told when he comes back? How can somebody return from where he hasn't gone in the first place? f I took more rides like this one, I would come to know why we are often treated as little children by the authorities. Such rides might also offer me an opportunity to investigate why the whites in our society appear to be more concerned with our welfare than we ourselves are. I would also like to find out if there is any correlation between the time the train arrives or leaves the city, and the time a burglary, murder or kidnapping is reported. In fact, the fields of interest are many. But most unfortunately, I lack the means to transform my wishes into horses.

Another curious phenomenon I would like to investigate, horses or no horses, is rumour-mongering. We the people of "Africa In Miniature" seem to love hearsay with all our might, heart and soul. I might for instance be devoid of almost every bit of information if hearsay were to be decreed outlawed. But why should rumour-mongering be so fashionable here? I wonder how many of my compatriots stop to ask themselves this question from time to time. The fault must be with the government's information policy. I hear that the policy is so restrictive, and that journalists are so tightly controlled that everything they publish or say has to be trimmed and pruned to suit government's taste beforehand. The role of the editor is played by the District Officer, who has been provided with a gun to kill stories, articles or dummies that are potentially offensive to the system. The Minister of State for Law and Order is renowned for his sporadic circulars, withdrawing this or that paper from the kiosks, or banning this or that person from practising journalism.

In the light of this atmosphere, one can understand why we are obliged to turn to the only other alternative available for news about our very own country. Frustrated by the national information system and alienated from happenings we would normally consider it our right to know of first, we turn to the foreign press. Since very few people can afford the expensive foreign newspapers, sketchy and distorted though they might be in the treatment of issues of concern for us, the majority of us are either left completely uninformed or informed through hearsay and rumour only.

Thus a political prisoner might be tortured to death at the BMM ('Brigade for Mass Murders'). The foreign press somehow comes by this piece of information and sensationalizes it by writing "A case of serious human rights abuses in Cameroon" ("Une grosse violation de droits de l'homme au Cameroun"). A frustrated Cameroonian journalist might capitalize upon this. He might tell his less fortunate countrymen (if he has a way) that the government daily murders its opponents in thousands: "Yet we Cameroonians are ignorant of the fact" he might stress. Then he might ask the rhetorical question: "Do we need a foreign paper to inform us of gruesome murders and rights violations that daily take place around our very noses?" And he might accuse the very foreign paper that is trying to inform us of complicity. He might criticise that instead of informing us, the paper was in fact bought over by the authorities to conceal some of the information by understating the facts. And he might make us believe that what the paper reports is nothing but the tip of an iceberg. He might be wrong, he might be right, but who can say?

Consequently, a government that might have lasted is forced out of office through a popular coup d'état. I believe that the information policy of any government in a way determines the popularity of that government. Leaders must never be impatient with their people's thirst for information. Nobody is a child; we can always choose what to believe and what to take with a pinch of salt. The danger of trying to control and filter information is greater than the danger of making information freely available. When a people's thirst for information has been subjected to Pavlovian whims and caprices by a government that is selectively informative, they tend to believe everything that comes from alternative sources. So if I were asked to advise the authorities of our triangle, I would say most insistently: "Let people know, they will always distinguish between Utopia and reality, falsehood and truth, for they are far more intelligent and responsible than you in positions of power are ever ready to admit."

I believe that if the government fails to act fast – and I sincerely pray that it doesn't –, it will not only be unable to curb rumour-mongering and slander, but be destroyed by it as well. These two diseases have eaten into our society like canker worms. However gullible we have become, there are some rumours that one finds so difficult to swallow. How is one expected to believe for instance that his Excellency the President has mistresses and illegitimate children sprinkled all over the national territory? I find it impossible to accept the allegation. I just can't imagine that this man of power, who instils such fear in everyone and whose eyes can hypnotise even the army general, is so cheap with women! The strongest of these stories is one which alleges that the President has a girlfriend who runs a "circuit", a beer and chicken parlour, so to speak. This beautiful girl is said to have been ordered by the president to poison her young husband. This she did and the young man is gone for good. Once he knew she was free from her conjugal bondage, the President started to visit her sophisticated parlour twice a week: on Wednesdays and Sundays. Since then, it is claimed that whenever he is about to call, he buys off all the customers for the evening. In that way the parlour stays closed, and the proprietress sits in waiting for her boyfriend.

The president drives himself in a bullet proof Renault 30 car. Nobody accompanies him. He is disguised when he visits his widow mistress. One day he overslept and got up when it was already day. He knew it would be risky for him to drive back. Everyone would recognise the presidential car, and eyebrows might be raised. The guards would be stunned to see the President they had thought was quietly asleep in the palace. He knew just how dangerous it is to give one's guards the impression that one is vulnerable. So he did something dramatic. He reinforced his disguise and took a taxi on hire, leaving his car at his girlfriend's. However, the taxidriver wasn't deceived. It is difficult to deceive anyone about the looks of a President who has been in power since Cameroon was first discovered by the Portuguese!

When the President realised he had been recognised, he signed a piece of paper which he gave the taxidriver to take to the minister of National Education and Superior Endeavours. Then he cautioned the driver against sharing the official secret with anyone. The latter saw the minister who acted promptly. He was given a scholarship to study Business Administration in France. He would return qualified enough to be made Managing Director of AVOC, I suppose. And that is how people make their way up to the top in this society. It isn't really merit, all depends on luck, and perhaps on how well you play your cards while dancing to the tunes of the Republic's Praise-Singers.

What I would like to know is the identity of the person who started this rumour. To me it is all fabricated, an expensive joke that would cost its author a pound of flesh and blood if the president should hear of it. Could the young widow mistress or the fortunate taxidriver have boasted to their associates despite all the promises made? Despite what they both had at stake? It's difficult to say, but possible all the same. There are many other rumours involving the president and other women. But I don't believe any of them. Like the one for example that it is no coincidence that the female members of his cabinet are very charming and almost always unmarried, or divorced shortly after they are appointed.

I think these rumours are just part of the price many people are obliged to pay for being great, rather than for giving the impression that they are great. A person has to be – or be seen to be – of a certain social standing to be earmarked for comments, rumours and calumny. But what an irony that these very people don't realise the truth. But do they care, does wind of all these rumours ever reach them? How do they react to such ludicrous stories? Perhaps some of them have a feeling of achieving purpose, a sort of greatness, a sense of conquest! So far so good for the President. Rumour or no rumour, I know it is my noble duty as a citizen to respect him, respect him for life.

There are other rumours about other people. These concern certain important but notorious individuals. What else do I expect to hear about members of government and managing directors of public companies with unprecedented records of mischief and promiscuity? If a member of government is attacked by a pregnant girl at the city centre in broad daylight for forsaking her and the baby he promised to care for, would it surprise you to hear that two weeks later he was caught in the act at another girl's flat, given a thorough thrashing by the legitimate boyfriend, and escorted to hospital in a Mercedes 280 SE with a broken windscreen? Or would you be surprised that another minister, visiting the city of Douala, was so mean that he was nearly humiliated by a stubborn prostitute? The rumour in the latter case is that Minister X invited a beautiful Anglophone prostitute to spend the night with him in his hotel. In the morning he gave the girl fifteen thousand francs, far short of his ministerial status. The girl refused to take the money, saying it was too small an amount for her to use to purchase anything, not even a bottle of "eau de toilette" or perfume. She threatened to scream if he refused to pay her a reasonable sum. Frightened by the prospect of a scandal, the said minister accepted to pay her the hundred thousand francs she had asked for. Who has forgotten the story about the minister of state who ordered his thugs to eliminate the mother of his illegitimate two-week old child, because she dared to remind him of his moral obligations? And there is also the story of a man who is said to owe his position, as director of a ministerial department, to the fact that his wife agreed to make love with the minister who is first cousin to the President. And so on and so forth, rumour, rumour everywhere!

My group is the second to be transported by this particular bus. I'm quite happy to go second. Call me a second rate citizen if you like, but do nothing to make me one. For I simply gave up the first trip to show how modest I am. Being among the first to arrive Bastos would have given me a false feeling of importance. It would also have made the place even stranger and more embarrassing to me. Going in the second group, I am more comfortable to think that some people are already there and that I'm just one of the faceless members of the congregation.

It is good to learn from the mistakes of the Humpty Dumpties, isn't it? But how many people do take the time to do that? How many ambitious soldiers in Africa for example ever learn from the personal tragedies of their unfortunate counterparts? Isn't it true that if they did they would take time to organise their takeovers and thus avoid the great number of lives often lost in the process? Year in and year out intellectuals are deprived of their right to liberty by the governments of their various countries, yet it would never occur to them to save their souls by relinquishing subversion. African leaders know for instance that the best way to obtain foreign aid is by abandoning Non-Alignment. Yet see them persistently hanging onto this high sounding nothingness, while more realistic Third World dictators elsewhere make giant strides away from this nightmarish third-worldism. African students know full well that no history book has ever recorded a successful student strike in their continent; yet every now and again they go out of their way to encounter the repressive police and the armed forces by striking for political and social changes. Wouldn't urban critics, for instance, be saving their lives by behaving with the voicelessness of the illiterate peasant masses of their various countries? So we must make a desperate effort to learn from the mistakes of others. Essential ingredients for the construction of the future lie in history, more than we are prepared to believe.

I'm not arguing for any endorsement of things the way they are. Far from it. I'm arguing that change is so necessary for us now that we must not waste our efforts on trifles, half-baked alternatives, or immature sporadic attacks on the present order of things. For these further weaken us, and make change even harder to come by. What we need is collective effort, a massive movement, sweeping mobilisation, and above all an impeccable sense of priorities. At the moment we spend valuable time substantiating mediocrity, rather than working towards authentic change. That is my position, and that, perhaps is what God has called me up to do – to coordinate our efforts so that the change we've sought and seek might come once and for all.

Our driver is very careful and experienced. He must have learnt to drive during the multiparty era when the situation in the former West Cameroon was even more sensitive and political candidates were extra concerned about their lives. A while ago I overheard him telling the man on his right how he suffered when he first adopted the French system of driving on the right. He says it took him quite some time to make what he terms "this worthwhile change". He claims that among all the things he was forced to abandon of his former English way of life, only the abandonment of the driving system was worth the pains. All the others were worthy of being emulated by his French speaking counterparts on the other side of the River Moungo. But it was unfortunate that the latter were quite unprepared to make any sacrifices, no matter how legitimate. And what could they, the Anglophone Cameroonians, do to enforce their point, when the Francophones outnumbered them so overwhelmingly?

Drivers like this one are never easily parted with; their employers would love to keep them for as long as they are willing to stay. He must be driver to one of these English-speaking Honourable Vice-Ministers around the place. And I know that to drive such a personality is not the affair of every Tom, Dick or Harry.

I am contemplating learning to drive as well. In fact, there are many things I would like to do. For example, I would like to practise martial art and judo for self-defence, realising that people must become increasingly aggressive if they are to survive. Although I spend days elaborating plans, my feet finally never leave the ground; not that I'm lazy, but I lack the person to give me the initial push of encouragement. Ever since my beloved mother died in an attempt to bring forth my sibling and father died of grief a few months afterwards, I have hardly had any real encouragement from anybody. And so my hand-to-mouth way of life.

I still recall the poem I wrote after their deaths. A poem that has come to mean so much to me. A poem that would fetch me the first prize in any poetry competition. I'm proud of it, very proud indeed. Whenever I recite the poem, I can still see my mother struggling in our house in the village, with no maternity assistance whatsoever. The village women were around to help, but what could they do when the child refused to come out? They tried the best they could, but fate had beckoned, and finally my mother and my unborn brother or sister (who knows what sex?) passed away. And so my poem, written in tears, and in the depths of my greatest emotional upset ever, remains the only thing that reminds me of these two human beings, to whom I wish life had been just a little kinder.

Titled Sharp and Brusque, the poem reads thus:

A sudden wild disastrous drop
In her farm beside a lively crop
Which she had hoped to reap by dusk,
Forced Mother to end, sharp and brusque.

Father and I cried, sobbed and wept
Day and night where her corpse was kept
Till tear-pools showed our pale faces,
And swollen eyes like round ridges.

Days went by as Father thought deep
Why I failed to eat, drink or sleep
When I knew the dangers so great,

Which he tried to enumerate.

Then with mixed concern and sad pains
Created by vile death's brutal stains,
Father went out to ease himself
And was asked to follow his wife.

Wicked, rash and foolish death was,
To leave alone in a big house
A little lone parentless child
With nothing to make life less wild.

This I write to let the world know
That they may not care to ask how
A little boy who was so sound,
Could vanish like a shallow wound.

In fact, looking back on my childhood years, I'm especially grateful I did manage to survive the deaths of my parents. I had a grandfather, my only relation in the world. But he was an old blind man who could only talk, and who never left the house. He was virtually no use to me (I must admit I owe my talkativeness to him, though), so I left the village as soon as I was ten and went to the northwest city of Bamenda, lured away by a young and active gang of thieves. I had to fend for myself, that I knew just too well. At Bamenda it didn't take long for the ring leaders of our gang to be caught and killed by an angry mob. Up to this day, Bamenda remains the only city in the country where the population has taken the law into their own hands as far as theft is concerned. They make sure they kill everybody they catch stealing, straightaway. The inhabitants of that city are ardent followers of the 'eye for an eye' doctrine.

I had narrowly escaped death, but was I going to survive? At first it wasn't easy, but eventually I was adopted by a sympathetic but miserable Bamoun family which had migrated to Bamenda in the days when the English were still in control of that part of the country. They sent me to school and were quite parental in their care for the three years I was with them. But when their own children became of school age, my adoptive parents asked me to go and look for support elsewhere. I could understand their position, for they were poor and struggled to make ends meet. I thanked them and left. When I came back to visit them a couple of years later, to thank them again and to say that life on my own hadn't been exactly as miserable as I had feared initially, I discovered that they had moved, leaving no forwarding address. It's a pity to have lost contact with a couple that was so nice to me. Yes, so nice to me during those early years of exceptional hardship. May the Almighty sprinkle some of His abundant mercy, love and kindness upon that deserving family, wherever they may be in this gigantic triangle called Cameroon.

Now we are driving through the rough and narrow streets of Briqueterie. The blind beggars have lined up the streets as tradition demands, Sunday being a day when all the shops downtown are closed. Despite this Sunday handicap, the beggars manage to quench their thirst and quell their growling stomachs by going from street to street and door to door with hats. Sometimes they are well received, but often they are poorly received. They are mocked by youngsters, manhandled by thieves, pursued by madmen, chased away by the violent dogs of the filthy rich in Bastos, and at times victimized by rain, a natural hazard. But they continue unrelentingly, with no disillusionment whatsoever, living up to the maxim that man should always struggle for survival.

Briqueterie is down in a valley while Bastos is situated on the elevated plateau just above it. The elegant houses of Bastos are European in style. Each is surrounded by giant modern fences built of concrete, barbed wire and broken pieces of wine and beer bottles. But down the valley the dilapidated structures of Briqueterie are half lying and half standing like banana trees after a heavy storm. These huts like little mushrooms are so desperately massed together that no individual can afford to build a fence round his hut without equally building it round the huts of others. People are compelled to live communally. Here in Briqueterie, if one person suffers all suffer; if I catch a cold, my neighbours sneeze; if the little dirty river at the west end of the village overflows its banks and causes a flood, every hut is flooded; and when the secret police raid in search of subversives, everybody is affected. The people have learnt to live together, and to enjoy one another's company. Thus, when it is time to fetch water, children rush to the public taps in groups; in the local school, they play together, avoiding to hurt one another; when it is evening, the men take their gallons to the oil stations situated in the Commercial Centre to buy kerosine; and when everyone is hungry, the women surround their smoky stoves to make couscous or boil some rice, for their families and neighbours to eat in little groups.

In Bastos there is no such thing as we find in Briqueterie. If the latter suffers from scarcity, the former enjoys superabundance. Bastos has light in abundance: in hedges, over the fences, in the grasses and on the trees. It is in Bastos that the National Gas company has ninety per cent of its customers. A company, which like the electricity company, has refused to have anything to do with

Briqueterie because its inhabitants are too poor to pay for any services.

There is the anecdote of a villager who came to town to spend some time with his son who had taken up a job with the "Ministry of Soya" at Briqueterie. The Ministry of Soya is a nickname given to a little open square in Briqueterie where a group of forty young men roast beef for sale 24 hours a day. The young men are self-employed, but they call their workplace a ministry because people might flood there to buy roast beef, just as civil servants are known to flood their various ministries chasing files and bribing their way through.

Early the morning following his arrival, this villager who had come to see his son went out and happened to stray up the hill to Bastos. There he spent the whole day, marvelling, moving from one sophisticated fence to another, watching the enclosed gigantic structures with primitive amazement. When by evening he returned and was asked where he had been the whole day, he said he had been to "the white man's country"! But when everyone laughed, he was rather annoyed and refused to eat anything that night. For he was serious in what he told them, that he had been in the white man's country.

Bastos isn't exactly like the white man's country, which is perhaps why the villager was laughed at by his son and friends. It might be pompous by Cameroonian standards, well built and thought to be heavenly and graceful, but Bastos is nothing more than a fool's exaggeration of reality in the West. Take the fences for example. I have expert information on this issue. Fences in the West have nothing in common with what we find here in Bastos, so I'm told. In the West the only fences that are as high up as the houses they surround, or that are lined with barbed wire and broken pieces of bottles, are fences around prisons and factories. Let no one think he can baffle me on matters concerning Europe, simply because I haven't been there. No way!

Isn't it a shame that the Europhiles of Bastos have got it all wrong on this issue? They have built little prisons for themselves in an attempt to imitate fences in Europe! Some of my folks here in Briqueterie might wonder, without knowing as I do, what the residents of Bastos have done wrong against their people and the rest of the world, that they have chosen to live behind barbed wire, protected by pieces of broken beer and champagne bottles? They give these folks the impression that they are living with their hearts in their mouths and make them wonder what on earth they are so afraid of. "The harmless blind beggars of Briqueterie whom their violent dogs have so far taken sufficient care of? Or are they afraid of the scrutinizing eyes of the wounded public?", the folks are likely to speculate.

Apart from the above, there are other phases of these two settlements which escape the eye of the visitor, but which strike the nightjar residents like myself. For to have a totally different picture of Briqueterie and Bastos, be resident at Briqueterie, and avoid being indoors after midnight. Then you would notice strange happenings. Top politicians and businessmen leave their Bastos residences at exactly 1 a.m. every night, and drive across to Briqueterie. Round about Hotel Coq they park their cars, then walk briskly into the side street and disappear into the generous darkness of the quarters. They penetrate the darkness into the various huts here and there, with a certain amount of precision that deceives no one. There, their political and business futures lie in the hands of the soothsayers, diviners or marabouts, whatever you choose to call the fortune teller. These men of the supernatural instruct their nocturnal visitors on how to behave throughout the week. They give the visitors amulets to attach to their underwear, concoctions to drink X number of times a day, and herbal lotions to wash their faces with. The visitors reward their venerated hosts, then disappear out of the darkness back to their cars and out into their light mad mansions in Bastos. All this they do between 1 and 2 a.m. Thence throughout the day Briqueterie ceases to exist for them again. Once more they pretend to look at Briqueterie with spite and condescension, succeeding in deceiving only their gullible Western visitors that the two worlds of Bastos and Briqueterie have nothing in common.

The Honourable V.M thinks his regular nocturnal visits to Briqueterie a top personal secret. When he goes there he drives himself. Even his dressing is unusual; he puts on a "ghandura" and a turban that identify him more with the religion and custom of his President than with his own religion or tribe of origin, whatever this is. He would definitely kill me if he but suspected that I know such a dangerous thing about him. If he could not succeed in killing me, he, I am pretty sure, would give all to make me keep the secret. Now that my financial crises are only increasing, I've been thinking on how best I can capitalize upon this piece of knowledge. However, time will tell.

We are now in the Honourable V.M's residence, all locked up like prisoners, but in merriment this time. The feast has just begun, and Dr T is introducing the main personalities. The Honourable V.M is named chairman of the occasion, Rev. Father Limbo who is now in a three piece suit is going to give the opening and closing prayers, while Mr S is going to coordinate the department of food and drinks. Only Prof. N is left without a thing to do, which isn't surprising because he sometimes gets carried away by bouts of mental gymnastics; and since no one knows when this might happen, it is better not to embarrass him in public by asking him to provide a service. On the whole the organisation is so smooth and we all look forward to the promised merriment. It promises to be unlike anything we've ever had before. I can't wait to start munching and sipping!

The priest stands up to give the opening prayer. He asks for silence which takes long to come. The Hifi is switched off. So is the Video, a rare commodity in the country. (I wonder when television broadcasting is going to be introduced. Cameroon is a chronic latecomer in the field of TV, isn't it? I wonder what the authorities are waiting for. Don't they know that elsewhere TV has always preceded Video?) Yes, the Hifi and the Video are switched off, but there is still some disturbing noise from one of the Honourable V.M's multiple bedrooms. It is the radio and it is news time. Nothing interests the Honourable V.M like news, especially news about Cameroon, news filtered through the radio. He likes Saturday afternoon news most of all, for obvious reasons. It is on Saturday afternoons that the radio announces all important decisions taken by the President. So ministers and civil servants all over the country have learnt to take their Saturday lunch with the radio by them. For they can be relieved of their duties, promoted or transferred from one area to another, just over the radio. Without being an expert, I know that in Cameroon the radio is a dictatorial medium, that has the powers to make people tremble and sweat, or jump out with joy and excitement.

Although it is Sunday today, the Honourable V.M is somehow very excited. He knows that the President of the Unified Republic has only just returned from a private visit to Geneva, and major shake ups are not totally out of the question. When you've worked with someone for some time, you instinctively know what he can or cannot do. The Honourable V.M asks the priest to suspend the prayer until after the news. The radio set is brought out of the bedroom into the hall and placed on the table. Everybody listens keenly to what is being broadcast, although very few can understand the news which is in French. All important news in Cameroon is in French, because the decision-makers that matter are Francophones. At the level of officialdom there is a ruling that where two texts seem to contradict one another, the French text should be taken as the authentic one. The implication is that if an Anglophone member of government writes a report which happens to be poorly translated into French, the poor translation would be taken to be authentic, while the real report is thrown into the waste paper basket. Yes, the news is in French, which most of those present can barely understand; but those who understand this language will explain to their less bilingual counterparts afterwards.

The Honourable V.M is very keen; he is even tense. The radio says that contrary to tradition, the President has judged it imperative to announce a cabinet reshuffle on Sunday. The Honourable V.M is completely changed. Why is he so afraid? The list is long. The hall is dead silent. All eyes are fixed on the Honourable V.M who is trembling with fear. Rev. Father Limbo is trying to calm him with "may God's will be done". Everyone seems to realise what is at stake. The party could well be jeopardised, I bet some have started to think!

The broadcaster has now finished with the long list of ministers and is on that of the

Vice-Ministers. This is where the Anglophones excel, in the vice-ministerial portfolios. There are altogether nine Honourable Vice-Ministers. The first eight names are all new to the cabinet, meaning that eight vice-ministers are replaced. The Honourable V.M faints at the seventh name; he is so sure he has lost the race this time. What must have happened? Did his marabout at Briqueterie fail to stir his magic pot or something? But he is far from being correct; the other eight Vice-Ministers might accuse their marabouts, but he still has some time to go. For his name ends the list; he is the last of the nine Vice-Ministers in the cabinet, but a V.M all the same. He remains an Honourable Cameroonian, and that is what matters!

A bucket of water is poured on him. The air conditioner is switched on. But the Honourable V.M is slow to recover. The crowd is petrified. The priest is asking for Holy Water. But there is none around; the Honourable V.M has never thought he could need it. Perhaps he has some only in his office. Everybody kneels down to pray to God for his sake. Rev. Father Limbo intones a series of "Hail Mary's" and "Glory be's"; he invokes saint Jude and saint Patrick, and calls upon the God of the Anglophones to save their son and representative. But the Honourable V.M shows no signs of recovery!

Then an idea strikes Mrs Honourable V.M the bush woman. She rushes into her husband's bedroom and returns immediately with an amulet and a bottle of castor oil mixed with potent herbs. The priest is scared and makes a desperate move to seize these from the humble lady. But she is faster; she places the amulet on the Honourable V.M's chest and pours some of the mixture into each of his nostrils. She knows her husband well, and has always loved him. As soon as she pours the mixture into the second nostril, the Honourable V.M, like a galvanised frog, springs to life again, full of vigour and worldliness. Rev. Father Limbo is stunned; perhaps now he will be obliged to revise his beliefs?

The Honourable V.M is told the good news. He looks around, appreciating the frightened faces of his concerned people to gradually get brighter once more. He is happy to know that he is still in charge, their leader today, just as he was their leader yesterday, and pleased that he will be theirs yet for sometime to come. He repeatedly makes the sign of the cross, muttering "my Lord and my God," and saying something I think his marabout must have taught him to say when under stress or faced with danger.

He declares a double feast. It's certain that tomorrow night at exactly 1 p.m., he will go down to Briqueterie and pay a well deserved thanksgiving visit to his marabout. For one good turn deserves another.

PART THREE

I've slept like a log. My head sways in the manner of a tall bamboo in a strong wind, indicative of unfinished sleep. I lie down again and enjoy the strange comfort of my bed for a couple of hours more. Then I get up once more, this time with a clearer head and a more agile body. Before I have time to think of where I am and how last night was spent, a gendarme officer suddenly appears at my bedside. His interest must have been arrested by my series of irritating coughs and sneezes.

"If you don finish sleep, we fit go I leave you for your house," he says with duty consciousness.

I look at him surprised, unable to recollect where I am and why I should be supervised by a "chef". There are no two ways of going about it, so I ask the officer: "Chef," I make sure I address him politely, knowing how much they like to be called Chef. "You fit tell me whosai I deh?"

"You no sabi whosai you deh?" he asks. "You sleep for fine bed so, waa, and you say you no know where you deh?" he expresses surprise, but my lost look tells him all. "Okay, make I tell you whosai you deh. You deh for the Honourable V.M's residence. You drank and get drunk and unable for go back home. So the Honourable keep me in charge to take

114

you safely back to Brique," he calls Briqueterie by the short but popular form. "So if you don finish sleep, we fit go," he concludes, showing me that he is ready.

This for sure is a good one. He takes all care to explain to me. He is very unlike many others. Perhaps he is specially trained to work with the Honourable V.M, and to make the world see the good side of the bad forces of law and order. I begin to doubt if I really needed to use the appellation "chef" in addressing him. He doesn't seem to be flattered by it, because he is definitely worth something without it. His counterparts would crush to death any civilian who omits the interjection while addressing them. They tend to think that they are actually great when they sound so, or when they literally push others to make them feel that they are.

I quickly get ready to be led away from this paradise. The comfort has been superfluous. I can by no stretch of the imagination visualise the magnitude of the presidency, if the residence of a "mere" Honourable V.M can already boast of this amount of sophistication. Here everything is in abundance: There are servants employed by the state to take care of the Honourable V.M and his family, gardeners to make the flowers blossom and clean and clear the yard, cooks and stewards to make sure that what gets into the Vice-ministerial stomach is the best, and chauffeurs to ferry the whole family around. Yes, the state ensures that its first servants are well lodged, well fed and well taken care of. For it really isn't that easy to be one of the first servants of the state! Here too, like everywhere else in Bastos, there are lights on hedges, grasses, and tress, that freshly bring to memory the wordings of a poem I once wrote opposing the two worlds of Briqueterie and Bastos. It goes thus:

There were compounds sad and dark
Which I passed onto the park
Men that smiled day and night
Lived a life without light
In these compounds sad and dark.

But, towering high and bright
Stood a lone house, mad with light
Light on hedges, grasses, tress
Made a man live in peace
Here, towering high and bright.

It is the second of the only two poems I have ever written. I have never given it to be read by anyone. But I truly believe it to be a good poem because it is a faithful transcription of my genuine innermost feelings. Like the first, I'm quite convinced of its unbeatableness in any literary contest. But I have been led to the unfortunate conclusion that poetry is not being given the place its due in Cameroon. Perhaps I'm the only one so far to know that a poet, unlike all the other types of writers, is like a mole that can never be stifled or trapped; his arteries of expression being as many as those of the latter. The subtle creative imagination of the poet makes him as ambivalent as a mask from the Grassfields.

The officer and I get into a waiting car. I recognise the driver as the man who drove us here yesterday, and wonder how he must have received the shocking news of the cabinet reshuffle. If his direct Godfather was one of the eight other Anglophone V.Ms that has been sacked from the cabinet, then the Honourable V.M might have to look for a new protector and employer for him. I can almost swear that is why he is sticking around here. With his master gone, his only real hope of staying employed is the Honourable V.M. And what a lucky man the latter must be, to have narrowly escaped the vicious axe that slashed away the eight other V.Ms. He for sure is going to miss his colleagues very much, and it would take quite some time for him to become used to the new Anglophone V.Ms in the cabinet.

I can see that the driver is as sober as he was before the feast. That is what I can't understand. Even the officer is sober. Does it

117

mean that these two don't drink alcohol, or that they have eventually come to master it? It must be that unlike me, they have already come to terms with alcohol. Isn't there always a difference between an initiate and an innocent?

We soon reach my street where the stench of rotten beef fills the air. My companions are discouraged. They would have driven in a little farther, all being equal. But today is Monday and the butchers are ready to turn capitalist. What happens to those who eat their rotten meat isn't their lookout at all. The golden principle is that they must refuse to recognise that market things can perish before they are sold. So they shout out with confidence: "Meilleure viande, meilleure viande"; "Fine, fine meat, fine, fine meat"; "Buy one kilo take two"; and so on, chasing thousands of fat dark flies away with little branches tied together to form bundles. And there is much effective charm in their words and salesmanship. Buyers come with handkerchiefs over their nostrils, and go back with meat in their baskets. Their families would eat and survive, for God takes care of them.

The driver reverses the car. I come down and begin to struggle through the muddy meanders that I'm so used to. Just then I hear a call from the car again. It's the driver calling for me. He walks towards me, a basket in his left hand.

"How can you forget a thing like this?" he asks with a smile of surprise.

"What's that?" I reply, trying hard to guess.

"It's true you were very drunk last night!
The Honourable V.M prepared a basket of presents like this for each and every guest to take home. This is yours." He hands it over to me and hurries back to the car, forcing me to strain my voice in an effort to thank him.

The basket contains a variety of well-made chewables, a bottle of whisky and a substantial number of soft drinks. I'm overwhelmed. Once in my room, I bolt the door (although it is full of holes, and anyone outside can still see through) and eat some of the food, and drink a bottle of Fanta to replenish my energy. Then I lie down to ponder over last night. My mind is now very clear. Three episodes stand out most distinctly: the feast, my chat with the hilarious Honourable V.M and my dream just before dawn.

I would like to know why I got drunk. Why couldn't I stay sober and keenly observe what others did? The exercise was good when I started it, why did I abandon it halfway through? What a brilliant opportunity I missed. I will never forgive myself for the alcoholic blunder of last night. Alcohol is often like a screen where one projects his illusions, but which blinds him to the world of realities beyond the glass in front of him. I have always thought that unscrupulous politicians can use alcohol to stifle opposition at every level. All they need do is encourage the proliferation of breweries, curtail the amount of money paid as tax by brewers, and lower import duties on foreign wines, spirits and beer. In this way they can retain their leadership positions for decades, since fellow countrymen and potential rivals would waste their talents away in great pools of alcohol.

Although alcohol is so readily available in Cameroon which also happens to be the world's leading importer of French champagne, I would hesitate to think that the government uses it as a political weapon. But there are others who think that it does. Why, they would argue, does a government that has a strong Islamic representation, encourage the proliferation of breweries? Would the government want Cameroonians to believe that alcohol is bad only for people of a certain religious and cultural background? If there is ample evidence that Cameroon is an example of a society where authorities encourage drunkenness in order to disarm its critics as some people hotly claim, why is it that some of the heaviest drinkers in the country are those in authority themselves? Last night I saw the Honourable V.M empty a bottle of whisky in less than no time, didn't I? And I have been told that cabinet members are each expected to spend no less than 300,000 Francs a month on champagne alone! Even the President, a professed respecter of the Koran and what it stands for, is said to take at least three bottles of brandy before each of his marathon orations! How would the proponents of the drunkenness theory resolve this apparent contradiction?

As I say, last night's party was interesting when it started. And I did some observation, countenance reading and mind searching before eventually losing consciousness. The atmosphere was quite ripe and those present quite conducive. I used my eyes and ears well for as long as my sobriety lasted. And what I saw and heard, imagined and felt, made me richer in experience. Yet some of it was quite unexpected and strange to me.

After a prayer by the priest that was hardly followed (I could see all eyes were focused on the central tables where the food and drinks were), the crowd fell on the food like a band of starving pigs. Some people couldn't believe their eyes when they saw the amount of food and drinks provided. They were silly to express such astonishment, for the Honourable V.M, Dr T, Mrs S, and Prof. N are not the sort of people one can underestimate. Moreover, the Honourable V.M had just been retained in the cabinet. This is a reality of which everyone in the hall was conscious. Then why did they struggle for the food? Perhaps it is an inherent practice – fighting for things even when these are abundant. The Honourable V.M had to intervene personally to stop the jostling, assuring everyone that they would have a fair share of everything. He therefore implored the crowd to be orderly and civilised.

Even then there was a gentleman, a Director, in a three piece blood-red suit worn over a white shirt and tie, who behaved quite unbelievably. He appeared to lack confidence in the Honourable V.M, for he failed to cease fighting. He forced his way through the crowd to the portion of the table which contained chicken, his cherished delicacy, I suppose. Unfortunately for him, just when he stretched out his hand to pick up a piece, he was pushed from behind. He fell forward into a large pot of yellow Achu-Soup. His shirt and tie changed colour as thick soup dripped from his hair, nose, ears and eyelids. Even the priest couldn't help laughing, although he made a sign of the cross immediately after doing so. There were jeers of "black man, black man, na so black man deh. He like chop plenty," from the crowd. And when this Director, as I was later on made to understand, asked his driver to take him home, the driver was too humiliated to accept. At that he was dismissed instantly. Perhaps the Director would have divorced his wife as well if she were present. It is unlikely she would have cherished an Achu-soup husband. Sympathetic Dr T finally arranged for the dripping Director to be taken home. I smiled at the thought of the ensuing domestic saga with his wife. But I hear that the majority of women are quite immune to embarrassments from the "superior sex".

Come to think of it, the humiliated Director suffers from a disease that is in no way uncommon. Fighting for services and favours is a widespread phenomenon in our society: In banks top civil servants and businessmen daily jostle for places at the counters; in the ministries and administrative offices, civil servants trample on the feet of one another, to be the first to bribe their files or dossiers through; vehicles struggle against one another to dominate a portion of the awfully narrow streets; buyers and saleswomen fight for convenience in marketplaces; the busy masses practise the law of the jungle at overcrowded bus stops; at the stadium football fanatics stage and play mini tournaments before the real and main; in nightclubs and drinking places, men almost stab one another to death over girls they haven't even approached; in the dungeons, political prisoners fight amongst themselves to delay facing the sadistic torturers; and so on and so forth. The questions that repeatedly come to mind are: Why are people always trying to take advantage of one another? And why, if my fellow countrymen are really as busy as they make believe, do we remain tethered by the arbitrary cord of underdevelopment?

I have no answers to the first question, and as concerns the second, I can only guess. Perhaps no one is ever doing the right thing. Perhaps people should not struggle to outmanoeuvre one another; rather, they should fight to overcome problems common to all and sundry. They should abandon the obsession to take advantage of situations and one another. However, others have suggested it might be because we lack confidence in ourselves and in our capabilities, because we have cultivated the crippling habit of imitating others, and poorly, so we remain largely underdeveloped. We virtually mimic other societies and their ways, never stopping to think out the implications of doing so, because we lack self confidence, because we have no minds of our own. What an attractive thesis this is!

There is no doubt that underdevelopment is a complex problem for which I can't pretend to have a solution. Underdevelopment is one of the few areas where I know nothing, which is a pity because I love being all round. It is an area that demands effective study by experts. Perhaps I should talk to that Dr B the senior lecturer at the Department of Sociology, that genuine intellectual who told Le Père Jean Mouton a bit of his mind. Yes, I should talk to him. He is quite lucid. I can see a bright future for Cameroon through his eyes! Maybe he has already studied the phenomenon in question. It is very possible, and his hypothesis might have been: "If Cameroon is underdeveloped, if Cameroonians jostle, fight or struggle for services and favours, it is because of the status of subordination, dependence and fatal expectancy; and the alienated mentality that decades of colonialism and neo-colonialism have imposed upon the country and people." I can swear that such a study would win him the status of a personna non grata all over the occident. But I think that if Le Père Jean Mouton was very affected by the "no sheep no altar" maxim, it is because it told the bitter truth about the contact between Christianity and Africans.

Strange that I've not met the respected Dr B ever since his legendry confrontation with Jean Mouton! What has become of him? Why doesn't he come to church anymore? Perhaps when he came to church at that time of the confrontation, he wasn't actually coming as a church-goer normally would; instead he might have come to study the phenomenon of church-going in the capital city of the country. Yes, that is very possible. It is a common belief that many people come to church for different reasons. Hearsay holds it that every Sunday, there is at least one member of the congregation with a walkie-talkie, gathering intelligence on and measuring the level of subversion in the rest of the faithful. But if the senior lecturer studied the practice of going to church for non-religious reasons, what could his conclusions possibly have been? Perhaps he found out that many people go to church often when their economic and social frustrations are total or nigh total. Perhaps the church is simply used by many as a rendezvous point for extra church activities. He might have found out that politicians go to church in order to familiarize themselves with their electors. Or that students go to church most when their examinations are at hand. For sure, church-going is an interesting phenomenon for a sociological study.

There is a rumour that the National University is the spring-source of struggles, uproars and momentary skirmishes. Students are reported to disturb lectures, jeer the authorities, scramble pell-mell for food at the restaurant, and carry home school furniture and utensils. I hear that they are condemned and termed vandals for doing what they do. But I know that institution well enough through reading what the papers say of it from time to time, and also by the country's number one way of getting informed – hearsay, to reject the condemnation of the students. A critical look with the sociological eye of the senior lecturer would give us the following hypothesis: "If the academic atmosphere in the National University is poisoned by seeming vandalism, it is because of the overweighing nature of the collective frustrations of the students; frustrations epitomized by the mystification of academics and its means of self-propagation."

Sometimes I actually venture too far! Why do I choose to meddle with issues that are above my competence? What has a mere Advanced Level holder got to do with matters of subtle academics? Does a nonentity like myself have the right to question the political set up of Cameroon?

How do I dare to think that the complex problems of today's world can be discussed by every Tom, Dick and Harry! What the hell is wrong with me! Who has cursed me with such a haunting "folie de grandeur"? Sometimes I wonder whether it was right for the Almighty to give me a hyperactive brain. It isn't good to be too intelligent, is it? Lord God, would you please forgive me for my inordinate ambition and blind determination to defy the traditional and sanctify anarchy. Forgive me lest I be reproached for "disrespecting the natural order of things".

After the Director's self disgrace, the feasting took a civilised turn. Order replaced anarchy. There was more than enough food and drink for all. And many of us ate for the past, the present and the future. That is to say, we compensated for what we've gone without, took advantage of what we were offered, and filled our tummies with enough food to take us right into the next day. When it came to alcohol consumption, the men literally asked the women and the children to sit aside and watch them excel. And what excellence it turned out to be for some of us! Alcohol consumption is like a secret society to which every male belongs; boys below a certain age, only prevented by harsh laws from becoming members. If it were a political party, it would enjoy the monopoly of government because all men would cast a vote for it; votes which a handful of feminine support would almost always assure a place of prominence in the political arena.

The Honourable V.M stood up to make a speech. I could tell it wasn't going to be a masterpiece because he had had so much to drink already. We stopped drinking, and the women and children ceased chewing and sipping soft drinks. He put down his glass and spread out his hands in the manner of a priest. But those with flexible minds knew he was imitating his political boss, the divine orator with a voice of gold, who always smears words with honey, embellishes them with an intermittent melodic cough, and rubs his hands with a hypnotic charm. Everyone paid attention to the Honourable V.M, who unfolded a piece of paper which he read out with difficulty.

It was what the masses would term a good speech; not because it was well written and well presented, but rather because it appeared to promise the fulfilment of past unfulfilled promises. Apart from many such cosmetic promises, the speech also contained an advisory warning – a word to the wise. We were told to watch against the inordinate ambition of the young and rootless upstarts of the society: "Everything in this world has its time; just as the children of today are the parents of tomorrow, so too are the led of today the leaders of tomorrow. The golden watchword should be PATIENCE," he emphasised. (Is it equally a truism that the evil society of today is the good society of tomorrow? Why hasn't the Honourable V.M paid attention to the quality of parents or leaders that the children or the led of today would make tomorrow, if the present order of things isn't reviewed and revised?)

He continued his speech, condemning the tendency amongst ambitious young men to abandon their own tribal names and take the names from the President's tribe in order to be mistakenly appointed into high posts of responsibility. (That was a good point, but why did he himself choose to go by the appellation "Honourable V.M", rather than his own name? He might say that he never asked anyone to call him so; but what has he done to dissuade us from addressing him by his title rather than his name? Nothing, as far as I know.) He uses himself as an example to illustrate the fact that in the system, people still have what they merit and merit what they have. The alcohol was making some people smile cynically without actually being able to say why. The entire hall clapped as usual, and hailed the Honourable V.M for making an excellent speech. He was as good a speechmaker as a minister of state, if not better, they flattered him. He must think of working his way up two steps higher, his friends advised him. They would all love to see him raised to the level of minister of state in the next cabinet reshuffle, which, as far as they knew, could well come up in less than three months. Yes, I remember, Cameroon is known elsewhere not only as "Africa In Miniature", but also "The Land Of Reshuffles". For what reason, I know not.

The speech over, the Honourable V.M regained his seat and the drinking, chewing, and chatting resumed. The festivity went uninterruptedly on. Everyone enjoyed himself, and some people wished they could have a feast every day. It is common in a society which capitalises on consumption rather than production, for people to think in this way. Many people are more interested in what goes down their throats here and now, than what they are going to eat and drink tomorrow. Investment is perceived as a sign of greed, not responsibility. And to sustain their philosophy of "wasteful consumption", my dear country has coined a saying that: "One must not postpone till tomorrow what one can eat today, for life is too short." Which is why even a drunkard lying helplessly by the roadside, would justify his state: "Why shouldn't I eat and drink my money? What happens if I die tomorrow?" some have been known to say. It is a shame that this country is infested with people who are too greedy to die leaving money behind for others to inherit.

✰ ✰ ✰

Yes, the Honourable V.M was right; the practice of adopting names for convenience is so widespread. Circumstantial naming has become a strong determinant in the process of social mobility in our country. There is the anecdote of a young man who continued to fail the entrance examination into the Higher School of Contemporary Politics until the year he changed his name to "Amadou Moussa". A journalist whose name sounded like a name from the tribe of the Minister of Information was made director of the national radio; a position he lost three months afterwards when the minister realised the journalist wasn't really from his tribe. "What is in a name?" Some persons may ask. "What is not in a name?" I would ask in turn. I know that there's much in a name. Call the name of a tribesman, a friend or a relation, and you strengthen my sense of security. Call any other name, strange or inimical, and you threaten the very foundation of my security. Which is precisely where I disagree with the Honourable V.M.

Isn't the President more likely to feel phonetically at ease with his tribe's names than with names from other parts of a tribally mosaic country like ours? But to change a name is to sacrifice a primary form of identification. A woman who takes up her husband's name on marrying him loses something of herself; her previous acquaintances can no longer identify her in the same way as they used to do. On the other hand, some might want to know of what practical utility is identification to one deprived of the pride and dignity of being a unique being? Tell them the essence of identifying one caged monkey from another, if you can. Identification, as far as they are concerned, has meaning only when there is justice!

I've learnt that it isn't only their names people change. I'm also told that fellow country men constantly find themselves forced to abandon their natural ages for professional and social reasons. They mutilate their years as need arises. Civil servants reduce their ages in order to qualify for the maximum possible number of years permitted to write a public examination. Students prefer to remain younger than 25 always, to avoid being denied admission into the academic beehive called the National University. The story is commonly told of a man who continued to reduce his age until a time came when he was two years younger than his first child.

Imagine how bemused non-Cameroonians who come to know of this phenomenon can be! "How does it happen? How do people manage to change their ages when one and only one certificate is delivered at birth," I can hear them asking. But it is easy to explain, isn't it? These certificates are drawn up by men, aren't they? And what is difficult in men undoing what they have done? I would tell any such bemused visitors of the saying that "The impossible is not Cameroonian" ("l'impossible n'est pas camerounais"); meaning that in Cameroon there is a way out of every possible entanglement. Concerning age, I would illustrate as follows: "If you were 20 and Cameroonian, and if you wanted to write a competitive examination into the civil service, where the maximum required age is 17, all you would do is to buy forms for the declaration of age which you fill, attaching a 300 francs fiscal stamp, and which you then take to the police or the district officer for a validating signature and seal. Within a day you would be issued a new birth certificate giving your new age." Wouldn't the visitor be stunned?

"That's just one instance," I would say, deriving some pleasure by telling him things that shock. "If you happen to be unsuccessful in the said examination, and would like to try your hand at another where the minimum required age is 30, you perform a similar exercise, this time raising your age to 30. The very same people who issued you a certificate of age reduction now issue you another raising your age. This time you might be successful, but your problems are not over yet; you might still need to change your age when you realise that with the civil service, compulsory retirement is at the age of 55. Somewhere along the line, when you think you've accumulated enough money, you would have to start bribing your bosses to put your file in order. You would like to be young again, so that you can stay longer as a civil servant and earn more money. And you can always succeed, if of course you know how to play your cards well, for nothing is impossible in Cameroon." Wouldn't the stranger congratulate me?

I have learnt never to blame anyone who behaves seemingly incomprehensibly, until I have fully understood what forces motivate him. This, I think, is the only way we can avoid prejudicing people for nothing; reproaching when we should in fact sympathize with our fellows. No one would naturally indulge in changing his age, without being pressured by the exigencies of life within his society. People hardly do things just because they feel like it. On the contrary, we are almost always forced into action by forces beyond our control. And those are the forces whose legitimacy I question. ...

The Honourable V.M was happy with all and sundry; he had a word with each and every one. When it was my turn to talk with him, both of us seemed to have so much to say or listen to. The others grumbled and complained that I was taking more than my fair share of time with the Honourable V.M. But all I would have told them is that it isn't always that the opportunity to chat with a dignitary knocks. There is an episode that occurred in the mid '60s just after independence and reunification. There was a cocktail party organised to celebrate the death of multipartism in the country. This party was attended by the President of the then Federal Republic, whose ingenuity and shrewdness were largely responsible for the new "unified" party. Everyone wanted to create an impression on him. He was new and the country he headed was also new; so he hadn't a clear-cut idea of what kind of collaborators he would finally settle down with. That day he was unusually late; his security men having delayed him with predictions of possible attacks, and so on. When at last he finally defied them and came, the general rush to talk with him was a mad one. The protocol officer had a difficult time keeping the surging crowd away.

But when the President met the Vice-President, he was so pleased. The two barely knew each other, so they spent the whole time conversing in Pidgin English; their only tool of communication. When at last the President thought that he could have a word with a few other persons, the protocol notified him that it was time to retire to the presidency. People complained bitterly, especially our Francophone brothers East of the Moungo. They hated the way the Vice-President had appropriated the President. Was this the way their Anglophone counterparts were going to make things difficult for them in this newly forged "Nation of nations"? It is rumoured that the ensuing protests were so bitter that the post of Vice-President was abolished, the constitution modified and the foundation stone for a reunified Cameroon laid. God bless that particular cocktail party that did much to change the destiny of this nation and to turn its constitution into a sort of working document ever after. May more party cocktail parties see the light; for we need more and more changes of destiny.

Perhaps I didn't simply monopolize the Honourable V.M last night. Maybe some great change is going to come out of our meeting. Lucky enough that no protocol officers were involved. So that he could always muster the time for a chat with others.

The alcohol was working miracles on me. I appeared bold and equal to the Honourable V.M. Take away his titles and you would have mistaken me as the superior breed, albeit in rags. That is why alcohol is suicidal; it ventures to make individual nonentities like myself ridicule the hierarchies of their societies, albeit like dogs which bark but cannot bite. I said things to the Honourable V.M that I wouldn't say ordinarily. At one point he pulled me into his bedroom. That must have been when I was blackmailing him. For I remember letting him know that I was aware of every single nocturnal visit he paid to the soothsayer just behind my hut in Briqueterie. Perhaps I spoke so loud that he feared others might overhear and subsequently spread scandal against him. I still think I saw him tremble with fear; but I can't say for sure, since I wasn't sober.

Before I faded out of the festivity into the underworld of the drunk, the Honourable V.M asked me to meet him in two days for an interview at the Vice-Ministry. Then he gave me 5000 francs which I'm unable to find now. Maybe that gendarme wasn't as good as he appeared to be. Maybe he offered to be friendly knowing the damage he had done to me. No wonder he smiled so broadly, appearing not to worry about the absence of the interjection "chef" in my addresses. They're all the same! He is a worse character, more malignant and cunning that Lucifer in the Garden of Eden! Quite ready to bite the very hand that feeds him. I would warn everybody to beware of all the "chefs" in this country, the smiling ones most especially!

Those in high places should be particularly careful. I mean those who rely on the "chefs" for direct protection in one thing or another. When power changes hands, its new wielders must always take the precaution to dismiss all the "chefs" that served their predecessors, if they want to reign in peace, unperturbed. Like hunt-dogs, these "chefs" are unfaithful to everyone else but their original masters. I have been told of some amongst them who wouldn't hesitate to stab their own parents in the name of republican peace! I can't deny the rumours that claim "chefs" are brainwashed with a sort of specially designed injection administered by doctors imported from France. It is clear that "chefs" demand a heavy price in return for being brainwashed, and for their unconditional support and protection. I've been forced by gruesome happenings in recent times to doubt if these "chefs" are sincerely honest with their masters even. They smile for as long as they are well fed. But when the masters become bankrupt financially, the "chefs" are bankrupt in loyalty. With them nothing goes for nothing. They are like prostitutes to whom the only thing which makes sense is money.

What assured me that the Honourable V.M actually meant what he said was the conclusive note of emphasis in his voice: "Do not miss the opportunity, Judascious Fanda Yanda. You seem an admirable young man." How flattered I was to hear him say this! Until then I couldn't have imagined him speaking of me with such kindness. Of course, I knew that he found my name 'Judascious' rather curious. The very first time he heard it was the day I offended him in church and had my ears pulled by his vicious thugs. I'm happy I was forgiven shortly afterwards. But my name was never forgotten by the Honourable V.M, who admitted that it made me not only appear like a Christian from the North of the country, but also like the wicked biblical betrayer of Christ. I hate the idea of being likened to

Judas Iscariot. Whom can I possibly be a traitor to? I'm neither in a position of power nor trust, and just how can I betray anyone, even if I wanted to?

I would like to declare my stance as far as treachery is concerned. I hate it as a point of principle and dislike everybody that employs it against others. I share everybody's belief that "once a traitor always a traitor". Therefore if a junior politician conspired with me to overthrow his boss, there would be no reason for me to believe that he wouldn't betray me in the same manner. Just as in social life, we must not think that a "friend" loves us when he speaks to us about others' Achilles' heels; for in the course of doing this, he is equally uncovering our own fatal weaknesses to prey upon afterwards when we fall out of favour. However, to satisfy the Honourable V.M once again, I did explain to him that Fanda is my surname and Yanda that of my late father, while Judascious is the cord which the priest who baptized me used to tether me to Christianity. In my tribe it is believed that a child is always his father plus something else, which explains why the child always adds the name of his father to his own name. Since the Honourable V.M insisted on knowing my tribe, I told him that I was born to a Christian couple of Bamoum origin. He was satisfied; henceforth, I wouldn't simply be known as Judascious Fanda Yanda which in the Cameroonian political dictionary means nothing. Rather, he would redefine me as the young man from Bamoun in the Nnoun Division of the West Province in the Unified Republic of Cameroon. May the Almighty replenish the Honourable V.M's satisfaction with my political identity.

I can't remember when I was bundled out of reality by superfluous alcohol. I don't know when the Honourable V.M left me, nor how I came to be found on the most comfortable bed of my life! I must have fallen asleep in the hall and been carried away to that guest room where I discovered myself today, and where that chameleon of a "chef" swindled me of a fortune! I would like to know if I behaved poorly when I was drunk. Did I use my mouth irresponsibly?: Meaning, did I say any silly thing to any woman, or did I make a subversive statement which might have been overheard by someone with a walkie-talkie? Did I dance in an uncoordinated manner? Did I lose control of my bladder? I hate the unconsciousness of which alcohol is productive! Certain more experienced drunkards avoid going off quick by putting their fingers right into their mouths in order to provoke themselves to vomit. This helps to clear the stomach, so that they can continue drinking again. They use such a strategy only when someone else is providing the drinks. I wonder how many people did that last night.

See how I can't even determine whether or not I betrayed myself and my cumulative frustrations. Did I speak freely about the political situation in the country? Why am I haunted by this particular question in this manner? Perhaps I did. I fear I did! Then I'm condemned! God forbid! To think of detention at the BMM is synonymous to thinking of death. I have never heard of anybody who came back alive after a period of detention in one of those underground hells called the BMM, not even the innocent victims who are imprisoned for months while the intelligence service works round the clock to find what could incriminate them. Often, by the time such prisoners are cleared of any subversion, they are dead and gone, killed by unjust torture and the thorny feeling of being imprisoned without a crime. But of what real political utility would be my death? What political tensions can the death of a gutter-citizen like myself quell? What use is it chopping off the limbs of someone already dead and gone? If those at the BMM had not become mere sadists that kill for pleasure, would they ever seriously consider eliminating a wretch like me?

I must be mad to think so wildly. Sometimes I actually lack basic common sense. Yes, I do. If not, why can't I realise that the Honourable V.M would definitely have thrown me out of his mansion, if I had dared to use my mouth irresponsibly? Let alone making insinuations on the political set up of the young Unified Republic! There is a human limit to everything. The Honourable V.M would not go out of his way to help me to his own detriment. No, never! Not even at the risk of being exposed and scandalised as one who visits the marabouts of Briqueterie. So I conclude that if excess alcohol had led to some irresponsible behaviour on my part, it wasn't such that should strain my relations with anybody. The living proof is that there was this apparently friendly "chef" who was assigned to take good care of me. If things had been otherwise, I would have been led away to the BMM, instead of being given a lift to my Briqueterie hideout, accompanied by a basket of presents. Perhaps only the "chef" behaved irresponsibly by stealing my money while I slept drunkenly.

The dream was long and frightful; it made me sweat profusely. I think it was a vision, for even when I forced myself out of sleep and switched on the lights, I remained deeply embedded in the strange world. I was confused, very confused indeed. "Why a dream like this? And why in the Honourable V.M's house? Why? Why?" I muttered over and over, my mind disbelieving what my eyes had seen. Strange things come not in strange ways, as we might expect! Great conflagrations begin from mere straw! Wasn't the first world war the result of a mere domestic quarrel in the Balkans? So it all happened in my dreams, which goes as follows:

The President of the Unified Republic suddenly fell ill, very ill. His situation rapidly became grave and he was evacuated to France for treatment. There he was told that over three decades of active politics had worn him down considerably. He had to relinquish politics to save his life and that of the country for which he claimed infinite love. So when he recovered and returned to the country, he freely decided to hand power over to his immediate subordinate and constitutional successor. Everybody hailed this unprecedented gesture; even those who would normally have preferred to have him cling on to the reins of power joined the chorus. But not long afterwards he began to move ambiguously, incomprehensibly. He began to covet the very power and position that he freely resigned barely a couple of weeks ago. He assembled tall, dark, diehard supporters with whom he held one conspiratorial meeting after another, swearing to bring down the very person he had named as "an illustrious successor". On his part the legitimate successor was baffled, but stayed calm.

Angered by the fact that Cameroonians were paying so much attention to this man who had all along been "a puppet to him" and that they condemned what he was doing, the resigned leader wanted to punish everybody. He invited international thieves and Soldiers-Without-Frontiers to wage war on his beloved country, kill every obstacle to a safe return to power, destroy all that took innocent blood thirty-five years to construct, and take the oil wells of Limbe and the gas deposits of Kribi as booty. In despair, he didn't hesitate to invite Moslem fanatics from North Africa to invade the country in view of forcibly converting everybody into Islam. He did ask, so it seemed in the dream, for bullets to be smuggled into the country in sardine cans. It was clear that he would stop at nothing to achieve a total comeback.

The country fought back bravely, protecting their new leader and the delicate institutional improvements that he had started to introduce. The people of Cameroon had seen a glimmer of hope in the change, and were very unwilling to turn the clock back. The aggressor was stunned by the unity that he had for a quarter of a century believed was superficial. Though more innocent blood poured, he was finally captured and caged in one of his very own dungeons. He was found guilty of activities "disruptive of the republican peace", and of trying to "subvert the institutions of the state," by a jury that was quoting from the very same dubious texts he had used against others for thirty-five years. The people's court decreed that he be punished accordingly, that he be given a lesson in his very own Institute of Torture, the BMM. Thus for the first day he was given electric treatment, whereby he was reminded of the presidential decree he had passed authorising the adoption of "la Méthode de courant", as this form of torture was called. On the second day "Les Gorilles" or the torturers suspended him on "La balançoire", another method of torturing – too complicated to be described, for no one subjected to it has ever come back to say how it operates – designed and used by the French in Algeria, and which the "subversive" President imported for use against his opponents. Early on the third day the torturers discovered him dead in his cell. They had come hoping to give him yet another lesson. Here was a man who couldn't even survive after experiencing only two of the multiple forms of torture that he had perpetuated for thirty years and more!

What a dream! What a vision! Could this be my long awaited signal from above? If yes, then it made no sense to me, for I honestly didn't know what part was mine to play in it. I didn't see myself play any part in the dream! I simply watched, like a passive spectator, hurt though I was to see all that went on. No, this can't be! I know I will have a major part to play when God finally gives me the go-ahead. Divine change will come through me; at least I was made to believe so when the Almighty appeared to me not so long ago.

However, I think I should tell the Honourable V.M to communicate my dream to his Boss, whom I wish well. He should do it, and not express fear like a cowardly toothless hunt-dog. The situation is grave and mistakes are likely to be fatal. I have never dreamt like this about an important personality before, so I can't say whether it is a premonition or not. But all I would like the Honourable V.M to tell his Boss is to be very careful. If ever he should come to a point where he has to give up power, which is very unlikely, judging from the ruthlessness by which he came to it, he should never, NEVER think of a second coming. For constitutionally, one can never eat one's cake and have it.

But if the President of the new-found Unified Republic should give up his bone just to jump upon it again, he would however not be the first to have shown such inconsistency in the world of power. History books speak a lot about leaders who abandoned the reins of power when they wrongly believed themselves too ill to rule or live. And how they came back burning, looting and killing, once they realised how grievous, painful and wrongheaded this decision had been! There is the pathetic example of a European monarch named Xavier XXIV who, two months after abdicating in favour of his son, came back with a group of mercenaries to seek the throne through the physical dismemberment of his son. May God forbid such political obsession in my dear Fatherland.

History also tells us of one such leader who was caught passing a bottle of deadly poison over to his successor's wife, intended to kill his successor. We know that he was caught and summarily executed. Why are people so unwilling to learn from History? Why do people appear so anxious to kiss the heels of oblivion about the exemplary past? Suppose, just suppose my dream were to come true. How sure can we be that the legitimate successor in question will continue to be good to the people, that his changes aren't just the cosmetic attempts so characteristic of people new on the scene? Why should we think that he would learn from History, when there is no evidence that any of his predecessors anywhere in the Dark Continent has? Yes, it's rather unfortunate that African leaders are not students of History. They would be in a position to learn that true leadership is achieved, not acquired; and truly speaking, one is never a leader, rather, one spends all one's leadership life learning how to become one.

If man is often too proud or reluctant to learn from man, why can't he learn from his supposed inferior, the animal? He would discover there is much to marvel about. He would for instance be struck by the fact that a dog might give up an old bone for a new one but ferociously wage war on any other dog that approaches the abandoned bone. There is also the hackneyed story of the dog with the bone on the bridge, which jumped into the water to seize what it thought to be another bone in the mouth of an enemy dog. Of course, in the fight with a nonexistent rival the dog not only lost its bone but also its life. Scarcely did it cross the dog's mind that what it thought an enemy dog was in fact its moral superior, his essence, so to speak. From this we might learn that man is his own worst enemy, and that greed may lead to self destruction. So whether from past leaders or from inferior animals, contemporary leaders have a lot to learn, if only they were willing.

Somehow students of politics have concluded that African leaders are permanently repelled by the lessons of History. It is claimed that they are blinded by their excessive love for power and the privileges of their high office. They are personally gratified to learn that the whole country comes to a gloomy standstill when they have a cold, or that work is ordered suspended and movements forbidden if they but venture out of their sumptuous palaces. I think these excesses are facilitated by the natural susceptibility of the human body. Does God need to order all celestial beings on their knees to be able to sneeze in a godly manner? Does the American President need to have the best material things in the US to be the respected personality he is meant to be? Did Gandhi of India cease to be seen as leader because he happened to have fallen in love with the virtue of self-abnegation? Is Nyerere of Tanzania (a very rare exception in Africa) not allowed into the UN and other world bodies because he lacks a foreign bank account and dresses only like an Ujamaa villager? Does ...? And does ...? A leader is the servant of the led; he is the number one servant, not the master!

Until of late I never fully understood why certain individuals would sacrifice even their wives in order to be nominated ministers. I was always struck by the willingness of many to be called upon to "serve the state". Now I understand! I understand that to be minister in Africa is like owning and operating a gold mine in Apartheid South Africa. Ministers know that they are there to help their Boss and his foreign facilitators to milk the rich succulent but naive cow that is their unfortunate country. They know that they could continue to be well off as long as they respect the apparently simple rules of the game: "Keep your mouth shut, keep your arms folded, learn to be blind even when your eyes would love to see, and know that your sole duty is to assure your Boss of total, unflinching and unconditional support. With all this done, rest assured of a terrestrial paradise." Nothing which appeals so much to human instincts can be easier to apply.

These rules are hardly ever written down anywhere. But whoever becomes initiated into the secret society of leadership is expected to learn them. Failure to do just that explains why the next cabinet reshuffle throws you out of the game. And you might never understand what your fault precisely was, unless perhaps you read an article on leadership in Africa or witness a conference by the Dr B the senior lecturer in the Department of Sociology. But that might never come because the sociologist's article and conference might never be permitted by the authorities. Imagine the most learned senior lecturer having to submit his writings to an illiterate (as most divisional officers are), for censorship! How is a man who can't even spell his name in French or English to be expected to determine what, written in either of these languages, is subversive to the system in place? Doesn't he run the risk of treating every word he can't pronounce as subversive grandiloquence? No wonder Dr B prefers to publish abroad!

Thus leadership in Africa becomes as sublime as a philosophical idea, which flies away when one is about to touch it. Both the intellectual and the masses thus find themselves in a vicious circle, in which they are helpless. Somehow I feel there is a way out; it is difficult to find a perfect vacuum in physics, or a perfect circle in mathematics. All the intellectuals need do is to be GENUINE. That is, be committed scholars and defenders of the voiceless. If African intellectuals have so far failed to have the required impact, it is because they often take refuge in the masses to foster their own personal ambitions, just like wearing a public helmet to run a private race.

Meanwhile let's confess one and all, in the name of the Father, the Son and the Holy Spirit that Democracy has failed to germinate in the "barren" soils of Africa. Often the issue of Democracy in Africa is presented as though it were merely a matter of resolving the ideological conflict between Unipartism and Multipartism. It surprises me that people should spend so much precious time chasing after red herrings. For, honestly speaking, pluralism is independent of the political system as practised anywhere in the world. Just as it is possible for consumer sovereignty in a capitalist society to be more mythical than real, so a plethora of political parties might mean no real choice or participation for the people. It would be simplistic and myopic to argue that Unipartism normally goes hand in hand with the lack of democracy. The real question is, how much participation and active choice are those in power (be it in a Unipartism or in a multipartism), prepared to ALLOW their people? Put in this way, the issue ceases to be merely one of an ideological warfare and becomes that of the faces behind the mask. May I remember to ask the senior lecturer for his idea on the "Democratic fiasco" in Africa, when I next meet him.

O! God, damn this restless spirit of mine, which like Hamlet's father's, will stop at nothing! What a terribly inquisitive spirit I have! Until I'm panged one of these days for undue intrusion, I will not know how advantageous it is to be blind to certain glaring absurdities. Two weeks ago I betrayed a robber who had almost thought himself off the hook. Nobody but I had noticed him, and just when he was getting ready to shout "Hurrah, Hurrah, I'm vindicated," I appeared out of the blue and opened the gateway into prison for him. He is going to suffer in there for a good six years! Yes, six years, and no less. French Law, I'm told; where the golden principle is that one is always guilty until he proves his innocence. How foolish in a way the French are! Don't they know that it could be quite a Herculian task trying to prove that one is innocent, even if one in effect is? Yes, that is French Law; strict yet shaky, and always freshly inspired by the ever young Napoleonic Code.

The noise often made of the Code Napoleonique (particularly in the periphery) sometimes makes me wonder what France was like before Napoleon, or how it would be today if Napoleon had been cheated of history. It makes me wonder most of all what French satellites in Africa would have done, they who have been rather rapid in abandoning their own authentic legal systems in favour of the embarrassing practice of branding people guilty until they can prove their innocence! Perhaps France would be comparable to a lawless jungle, if Napoleon had not done what he did. And French Africa? God alone knows. May Napoleon be praised for bailing the situation out in time!

I happen to love the French people with all my soul, despite all. Most people in French Africa love France. Paris is like home to most of us who can venture out there. The entire French territory is as dear to us as if we were actually French by birth. And what a great country to love! What a pace-setter! Although history has been somehow harsh with France, this country has always marked out the paces for real great nations to follow. I've heard so many sad stories about the futile missions of the French Intelligence Service in the rest of the world. But this in no way affects my love for a nation I personally think great. However, I would like France to reorganise its intelligence service so as to reassert their waning integrity. Perhaps those who accuse the French Intelligence Service of failures are hardly aware of its numerous successes in the continent of Africa. Who would deny that almost every coup d'état the French have organised in Africa has been totally successful? At least, let's allow merit to whom merit is due. It's a sign of open-mindedness, isn't it? My beloved France excels in the domain of coup d'état. Which might explain why the phenomenon of ouster is known world wide by the French expression of "Coup d'état".

This reflection on the French reminds me of an episode that almost slipped out of my mind. About a month ago I took the bus for Mimboman. In it was a man in his early forties. He was strangely calm and deeply in thought. He neither struggled for an empty seat nor appeared to be happy about his presence in the bus at all. I think he even hated his very existence. Something drastic for sure had happened to displease him so. I could see he wasn't attracted by the noisy gossips around him; but why wouldn't anyone who understood what the gossips were saying be keen to hear more? Maybe this man couldn't speak French, which to him might pose a serious problem. Perhaps he felt like a fish out of water. But who would this fish out of water be? An Anglophone of course! Who else should feel ill at ease with French in this great city? But Anglophones here are quite familiar with French, aren't they? At least they either pretend or are forced to be. Some, the soldiers and policemen in particular, are preferably more fluent in it than in English, their primary school tool of communication. An Anglophone soldier, gendarme or policeman would have no scruples making life miserable to his fellow Anglophones by speaking to them only in broken French. Some of them even refused to be recognised by former schoolmates, by insistently asking for travel papers in French, a language they barely know themselves!

I set my mind to work, and tried to decipher who this man was, before he could tell me himself. "If this curious fellow is actually ill at ease with French even here in the great city, then what type of Anglophone must he be?" I asked. Then proceeded to suggest an answer. "For all I know, he doesn't have the looks of a provincial Anglophone. Of course I know. He is one of those Anglophones who failed to treat our efforts at reunification with adequate seriousness. One of those who, frightened by superfluous French in the National University, fled abroad for academic salvation of some sort. He surely belongs to that class of graduates bred either in Nigeria, Britain or the USA. An exclusive product made in pure and uncontaminated English, the language of the Queen and Uncle Tom."

Just when I sincerely wished that this man would speak to disclose his identity, something happened that brought the two of us together for almost an hour thence. And I thank the Almighty for how much I learnt that day; a day I term great indeed. A ruffian who smelt of Indian Helm smashed his foot in a struggle out of the bus. So the gentleman cried out in English: "Hey you there! You don't wanna pull off my toes, do you?" But the ruffian was off and gone, as the bus continued moving. The gentleman was left alone in his anguish to solve his problem in the way he liked. Both of us occupied two adjacent seats that had just been abandoned by passengers who were ready to jump off at the next stop.

My neighbour continued to curse and swear in English. On hearing him speak English, I turned and faced him. He noticed my inquisitiveness and inquired: Are you English speaking?" "Yes, I am," I replied. "Happy to meet you," he said, quite enthusiastic, but still concerned with his hurting toes. After a few more complaints about the "rough frog" – a terminology I pretended not to understand – he started talking to me on more general issues. Soon the talk, which he entirely dominated, drifted further and further into a tense personal testimony. How sorry I felt for a man who appeared as an individual most embittered, and who found nothing virtuous in his country's politics and policies!

"This country has suffered too much under the yoke and whim of one individual," said my man, after declining to tell me his name, although permitting me to call him Dr Q. "It's strange how a people can allow its hair to be shaven with a broken piece of champagne bottle for thirty years and more. I know it, I know that people are unhappy, that they are disgruntled with the state of affairs. But what I can't understand is their docility and apparent acquiescence. Why can't they stand up and say enough is enough? Why comply as though they were subjugated by the powerful hypnosis of a French magician?" He smiled mischievously, and observed me to see if I shared his deeper meaning. I didn't, and I'm sure he read that from the blank look on my face.

"I vividly recall how the French cheated the true founding fathers of this country of history in favour of their nitwitted noodle and his band of praise-singers." Here I could guess those he was referring to as "the true founding fathers". It was whispered everywhere that the late Mr U.N had been a hero in his days. There was another hero whose name started with the letter W, but which was too difficult for me to pronounce. There was mention of a bishop as well. If all these people and many others were the heroes rumour claimed them to be, and if it is actually true that the French did cheat them of history, then steps must be taken to right past wrongs.

"Tell me," embittered Dr Q called my attention. "Is it because a man happens to be handpicked and placed to pilot the ship of state at the dawn of independence, that he necessarily becomes the founding father of the nation? On the contrary I think that such a man is at best the founding father of the neocolonial state! ..." He interrupted himself and took out from his pocket a handkerchief which wasn't exactly white, but which had the initials L.Q on it. This made me guess that he must be married to a woman whose name began with the letter L. He cleaned his nostrils and mopped his sweating face. I could see that he was heated up. This issue must be quite dear to him. "Yet we continue to lavish praises on him as if we didn't know better! The entire country is littered with absurd assemblies of praise-singers who are nothing but fruitless fig trees to their own people! How can things change if all of us are too scared to fight for this change? We all whisper with belittling complacency, 'it's the system, it's the system'. But that isn't true. It needs people to implant systems, and it needs people to do away with those systems. It's either you and I, here and now, or never!"

This man frightened me. His degree must be on the art of criticising. He was so pungent in his attacks. I tried to hush him down. He was endangering himself, greasing his way into the BMM. I feared for him. I wished he understood how dangerous and strangely uncommon his manner of freedom of expression was in our milieu. The individual he termed a demi-god and criticized so acridly and so vociferously was not dead; on the contrary he had never been more up and doing in his life! Moreover, this "false father" of the nation wasn't even out of the country. He was right there at the palace built for him by the French; built to resemble Louis XVI's Versailles residence. How then could Dr Q be so daring? Why did he throw all caution to the wind? Would he claim to ignore the fate of others, who like him had dared to go too far? I wondered if he were trained in America, where liberties are said to be plentier than the air we breathe, and where democracy can actually be harvested from trees like any other fruit; yes, America where I hear the words "My Constitutional Rights" are said an infinite number of times every second of the day!

"Why shouldn't I speak boy?" I would prefer to be tortured at the BMM than lose my freedom of expression. Thomas Jefferson once said that the tree of liberty must be watered from time to time with the blood of tyrants. What is happening here in Cameroon is that we've failed to water that tree for a little too long. The consequence boy, the consequence is that the tree is dying fast. It's our place to rescue it, and to rehabilitate it; then build a protective wall of iron round it, and with unthreatened joy, watch it grow, one and all." I admired the way he spoke, like someone I would trust, someone the populace could rally behind, to tell the "National Milkman and his International Counterparts" that the cow has been milked for long enough.

"Imagine boy, imagine that I have a PhD in Business Administration from a most renowned American university," he continued, with my deserved attention. "I return home to help develop my country, which according to Rostow is still five stages behind time. I have many bright ideas in my head and would love to implement them immediately. But can my documents go through? First of all, the "Bureau of Degree Equivalence" where no Anglophone is employed would not recognise my PhD. According to the Francophone chief of service in charge, my PhD equals a "Doctorat de Troisième cycle" – the normal equivalence of an MA – because I spent a fewer number of years than normal to obtain it. I've never known of a system elsewhere in which mediocrity is rewarded and excellence despised. Unprepared to argue with fools, I allow them to equate my PhD to the French MA, if that would please them, and if it would make them employ me.

"But they are so slow, and ask me to compile documents that are bullshit to me. I would rather they asked me to buy fiscal stamps worth such and such an amount of money. That would be far better than making me rush around in the hot sunshine, begging the police or the D.O. to sign ridiculous documents. In my file, you have certified true copies of my degrees. These take time to make, yet my employers would not accept photocopies, even with the originals available to testify that these belong to me. The most ridiculous of all the documents concerns the birth certificate. I'm asked to provide a certified true copy of my birth certificate, which I do. Then I'm asked to provide an extract of the birth certificate, and also to bring along an attestation showing that it is true that my place of birth is actually where I was born! It is clear that what they need are taxes. But by Jove, what a way of going about the whole business! I see these bureaucratic bottlenecks as a carefully implanted network to discourage progress and to blind every blessed son of the land with a clear vision of things.

"Naturally this worries me, so I try to investigate to see what the problem really is. Might it be that our young nation Cameroon is indifferent to the international calls for development? No! Far from that. The reason is that the French are everywhere in the country. They are a delicate people who must not be hurt. Or so they've made their unsuspecting stooges believe! Moreover they are experienced and therefore just the right type of people for Cameroon. Everyone knows that no Cameroonian, no matter how learned, can be a substitute for even a most elementary Frenchman. For as the saying goes, we are of a black skin, and we are trained by the French. And as you and I should know, not only is a black man naturally inferior to his white counterpart, but also the French believe that no student can ever be more than or equal to his master. They consider us as children who must be given paternal guidance. But whereas every other child might grow, it appears French children are never meant to grow. With the French "once child, always child"."

I decided to remain silent and just listened. This was an opportunity to weigh my ideas and beliefs against those of this weaver bird, before determining whose needed re-examination. I admired his insinuations and irony. Isn't it characteristic of the suppressed to be quite tongue-in-cheek when speaking about their oppressors? I prefer to think that is the case.

Dr Q continued: "The entire clique is a very intelligent one. I was told so many things, but never in a harsh tone. They always took their time to explain matters to me, nonexistent matters of course! Always overdoing it, I must assure you. I have never seen a nation which clings so much to its traditional errors and prejudices. Almost a century ago, Levy Bruhl and other Frenchmen encouraged colonisation by branding us: 'Peuplade à la Mentalité Mythique et Prélogique' for whom France had a 'Mission Civilisatrice'."

So he knew French after all? He was just being bitter about speaking it? I could understand his attitude, which was similar to the attitude of all minorities; a sort of way of fighting back. But I didn't interrupt him, because I was most interested in his story.

"Today," he continued, almost shouting, "despite all science has proven wrong, they still feel too insecure to consider us as fellow human beings. Cheikh Anta Diop proves with scientific honesty that Egyptian civilisation was the very first in the world, and that man first inhabited Africa. Yet the

French wouldn't agree with him, not because his thesis is scientifically invalid, but because "ça vient d'un noir!"

"And we the Blacks have really had a hell of a time with them. Here in Cameroon their heritage is great, their presence widespread, and all to be jealously protected. Always remember that as a people they are as delicate as eggs and must be tendered, cared for and protected against hostile competition from fellow whites or from their black inferiors.

"However, remember that having failed to do what I loved, I at least had to do something to sustain life. One must live, if one must fight for a better life. I therefore accepted the alternative they offered me. To sit behind a table in an unventilated little room – because I'm rankless in the civil service – and help foster development administratively. My goodness! The entire system is rotten, rotten as a very rotten egg! I can't understand how other intellectuals have ably borne it. Can you imagine how the stinking system functions? You are a civil servant, are you not?"

"No, I've never worked with the government sir," I replied.

"Do you have a job at all?"

"I have nothing worth the name of job."

"Then you are the veritable 'Damné de la terre'".

I must repeat that it came as a surprise to me that Dr Q could say some French words at all. But in Cameroon, French is by far the most intrusive language. It is like a cold in the Anglophone community. Unfortunate that the logic of numbers doesn't offer the English a similar advantage with Francophone Cameroonians. Again, I chose not to comment aloud on Dr Q's French; any comment might divert his attention. I liked listening to him; he had such important things to say!

"However," he continued uninterrupted, "let me tell you how functional a rotten system is. You would be shocked, quite shocked, I bet you. First, know that the academicians or intellectuals have no place of honour in this country. The satisfaction academic qualifications bring is illusory. I now understand why it needed a Frenchman like Sartre to propagate such a philosophy as "existence is essence". This simply means that the essential thing is to ascertain life, philosophical exercises are secondary considerations. Just like saying: "Live first, philosophize afterwards". If you were a student in the National University, you would have noticed that some Francophone philosophy lecturers, like in almost every other thing, have followed this French prescription to the letter. That is why each time the students are having diner, some of these philosophers who rear pigs park their cars outside the University Restaurant, ready to pick up the remains. Their maxim is: 'Mangeons d'abord, et philosophions après' – Let's eat first, then philosophize.

"With this typically French spirit, it isn't surprising that the true financial giants of the civil service are those who went through the parochialism of the so-called 'Écoles des Formations'. A primary school leaver who spends two years in one such centre of mediocrity earns four times the salary of a learned university lecturer who is derogatorily referred to as 'L'Assistant'. Whatever that means! But bear in mind that French nomenclature is the most ridiculous in the universe. You would be shocked to know the system. It's rotten as I've told you. Those with valid and widely recognised university degrees are employed as 'contractuels d'administration', meaning that they not only are going to have lower salaries, but are also going to miss a lot of fringe benefits reserved only for 'genuine civil servants' – 'les fonctionnaires'; those trained in the so-called 'Écoles des formations' – those who have a right to so much money because they happen not to be thoroughly trained.

"All this nonsense shows to what degree we are still dependent. Our infra- and super-structures are still alienated. The above categorization of workers clearly depicts the harmfulness of the French colonial system. It is one of the numerous relics of the French policy of the mediocritization of the colonised. The simple reason being that to ensure their domination and consolidate their orchestrated superiority, the French tried by hook or by crook to smother the ambitions and academic aspirations of their belittled colonial subjects. So they offered us an illusion of greatness by stifling ambition and open-mindedness with superfluous money. At the same time they injected into us an exaggerated craving to consume French. This was such that the sooner one abandoned pure or subversive academics for one of the centres for the proliferation of mediocrity – the most apt colonial tool –, the greater one's material benefits. The system is a vicious one characterised by the underlying propagation that academic pursuits, or the pursuit of knowledge in general is a futile exercise. If it were so, if all that mattered was a good salary, French wine and food, and Parisian dresses elegantly designed, if these were really all that mattered, why is that the very French encourage academics and the pursuit of knowledge amongst themselves back home in France? Why don't they join the bandwagon and carry mediocrity and consumerism to higher heights? No, they wouldn't do that, because unlike their naive black counterparts, they have never underestimated the power of academics. They know the importance of knowledge; they know just how effective a weapon academics can be against undue domination, against the marginalisation of the 'L'Afrique Noire'.

"But my problem isn't so much with the past as with the present situation. What amazes me is that we should still maintain such obsolete structures despite our alleged independence. Perhaps we want to tell the world that this independence was somehow premature, a sort of passing illusion. Then let's come out clear and do equal justice to both the French and the English. Let's even invite the Americans, the Japanese, and the Germans our pre-world war one colonisers! Let's ask each and every one of them to come and stake out for themselves portions of this generous triangle, where they can settle down in peace and start substantiating their own version of mediocrity. For Heaven's sake, let's be unequivocal with our invitation. Let's not invite them stealthily as if we were trying to play our population or a section of it a dirty trick of some sort!

"My dear brother, I don't know you at all, but let me confide in you. I have resolved to go back to the U.S. until things change for the better in this country. Until the river of change sweeps away the relics of colonialism I would never dream of coming back home. Thus when the winds of change shall blow open the doors of the BMM, liberating imprisoned freedom and justice, I shall come home again singing with joy:

"Home again, Home again,
I have seen my home again.
My dear mother Cameroon –
Let's join hands together
To remould what they tore asunder.
Home again, Home again.
I have seen my home again."

Dr Q said these words in such a slow and deliberate manner that I couldn't help thinking of them as a prophesy. Some profound belief and hope in future years. Oh! how necessary is hope! I actually saw it give Dr Q the courage to give me a farewell smile, and an "au revoir" as well. For at this point the bus stopped, and he who had almost forgotten that his journey was at its end had to leave me abruptly. He hadn't even time enough to give me his address in America. I'm convinced that he would have accompanied me to the next stop if he had a little money more on him to take a taxi back. How right are those who say that poverty is the breeding ground for illustrious ideas! It is almost as clear as water from the spring that Dr Q wouldn't speak with the same tone if he were better off. For there are certain things that have meaning only to those who actually live them, who experience them. How do you expect a princess to know what life in the inner cities is like, when she has never ventured out of the protective luxuries of her sumptuous palace? Impossible, isn't it?

I admire Dr Q and feel sorry for him. But I still can't understand why he preferred to go back to America. Wasn't that a somewhat irresponsible thing to do? I'm one of those who believe that the best way to fight for change isn't by shouting across the Atlantic or the Pacific, but by staying right here and opposing. Perhaps Dr Q might never venture out of the country after all. Given that was unlikely his first time ever to express his disgust with the system, he might have had spies following his moves and words. In that case, his passport is likely to be seized, and he might never be allowed to leave the airport. It is whispered that the Cameroonian Intelligence Service uses supernatural means to track down subversives. I had a feeling that the bus driver overheard all Dr Q told me and that he feigned ignorance of English in order to get the latter well entangled. In a country where nothing is certain, one always needs to plan with God. So if Dr Q planned with God, he might just have been able to sneak out to the US. But who can be certain with a security force that uses magic and sorcery to track down enemies of the government? And so I fear for Dr Q. I fear that he might well be languishing through his last moments in the stifling BMM. May his soul ascend into Heaven and rest in peace with God, even if his body is dumped in the River Sanaga.

No! I can't tolerate the next thought, palatable though it seems. Thinking, if left for long uncontrolled, can become an addiction. I think I'm in the early stages of that obsession already. But the addiction isn't exactly chronic yet, so I can still say enough is enough. My grandfather was used to saying that when an animal is young, soft and weak, people would eat it plus the bones. But I must tell these thoughts not to take my leniency for weakness. Moreover I'm still feeling very weak and tired. Alcohol can be so incapacitating! I can eat some of the chewables again, take some of the tablets a Nigerian smuggler-trader gave me a fortnight ago for housing him – which would prevent any headache developing –, then go to sleep. I

want to be clearheaded when I meet the
Honourable V.M tomorrow.

PART
FOUR

The Honourable V.M is like my blind grandfather, always criticising, yet unable to do any better himself. He sometimes makes me feel so ashamed of myself and my ways, yet never actually guilty. No, all this should stop! Things can't always go the way he expects them to! The world is not that monolithic. May the Lord render him less parochial. It surprises me that the President should think that such men as the Honourable V.M are so indispensable. Perhaps a cabinet means the agglomeration of the parochial, the mediocre or the unduly shortsighted and the deaf. If what I hear of the President is true, then I should expect no less shocking cabinet!

Some top critic of the government who once very narrowly escaped imprisonment without a crime is alleged to have said that the President once boasted in the late sixties that, "Cameroon would be stripped into nothingness by tribal sentiments" were he to abandon power. I consider such a declaration self-aggrandisement, pure and simple. What did the president really want to say? That Cameroon would cease to be when he ceases to be? Or that if Cameroon cherished its existence it must assure his, and as Head of State?

If the latter is what he meant, then he is likely to be suffering from the mental deformity known as paranoia. A man who speaks like that of his country can't be normal, can he? Rather, he should be a case for clinical psychiatrists to experiment upon. For an individual to wish the life of a whole nation to centre around his person is the farthest mankind can go in the direction of tyranny and self conceit! Perhaps that isn't what he meant after all. He might simply have meant that the country would be plunged into a real inferno the day its topmost executive would come from any other ethnic group than his own. But what does it change if this is what he meant instead? Would he want to have Cameroonians believe that colonialism by external forces has been substituted by an internal inter-ethnic one? Then the best he should do is to cut off his ethnic group over which he can declare himself President for life, but allow the rest of the country even a limited amount of badly needed democracy. For democracy is like sunshine to a plant: the more it has of it, the taller it grows, but the less, the more stunted it is.

Sometimes I wonder why the most respectable sociologist Dr B has not been made minister yet. He is the most lucid intellectual I know. He has a clear idea of what is wrong or right for this triangle. He writes highly intelligible articles and is always broadminded in approach. Since his confrontation with our former priest Le Père Jean Mouton a couple of years ago, Dr B has appealed to me most especially. I have never missed an opportunity to eavesdrop or read about him. What a prolific writer he is! He uses many forums to transmit his ideas. And how well he puts them! What a rich well of knowledge he must be!

I wonder whether what he says ever gets to the right ears. Like the article by him, which I cut out of the *International Review of African Politics* – banned as would be expected, but copies of which infiltrated the country, as would be expected too. It was marvellous and wonderfully appealing. I have pasted it up on the wall in my little room. I read it every morning and evening as if it were some sort of prayer. In a way it is, because it has reduced the number of 'Hail Marys', 'Our Fathers', and 'Glory Bes' that I say every morning. I think I will copy it out for the Honourable V.M to read. And critically watch his reaction. Will he understand? For now that remains a question. Perhaps I should copy it out straight away. There's danger in procrastination – the disease that killed Shakespeare's Hamlet.

International Review Of African Politics (I R A P), VOL.2 No.1 1976
"African Heads Of State: Traditional Or Modern Ruler?" By Dr B (Political Sociologist)

Political Scientists and Anthropologists all agree on what defines a modern state. One of the criteria they use to distinguish between a modern and a traditional state is the source of Legitimacy. (A government is said to be legitimate when it is conscious of a right to exercise power; a right which the governed recognise.)

Using Weber's models, in a traditional state authority is validated through the king (Fon, Lamido, chief, etc.), who bridges the state and the supernatural world of the ancestors. Because the ancestors are believed to be infallible, it is held that the closer one is to them, the nearer one gets towards being infallible oneself. Accordingly, the king would be the most perfect living person; and, as is to be expected, the lords, notables and the rest of the nobility would have imbibed degrees of infallibility, depending on how close they get to the king.

On the other hand, authority in a modern state is validated by well established laws to which everybody owes allegiance. Here the President (or Prime Minister), his or her ministers, and others are obeyed and respected not as persons in themselves but by virtue of the legality of what they order, and within the limits of the authority of their offices.

Thus, as concerns legitimacy alone, it is quite obvious from the above distinction that almost all fifty of OAU member states are in principle modern. And, but for a king or two, all the other African Heads of State would claim to have come by authority in a modern way: That is to say, either by popular vote or by popular coup d'état.

Whatever the case, the problem here is not very much how a leader comes to power, or what legitimizes his government. Rather, it is of interest to know how he behaves or, how he is treated when he assumes office. Is it like a traditional or modern ruler?

If the king (Fon, Lamido, Chief, etc.) often stays in office until his death, it is for two reasons. First, his position is incontestably hereditary. Second, because of his divine and sacred personality, his people consider him the salt with which life must be lived in this otherwise anarchical world. It is not because he is necessarily a despot, as many people have dared to think.

Like the traditional rulers, the African Heads of State often stay in office till they die either naturally or by way of coup d'état.

Because this attachment to power is neither legitimate traditionally nor rationally, African Heads of State nourish their ambitions most undemocratically and coercively. Thus, once in office, instead of thinking how best to fulfil the rising expectations of their peoples, these Heads of State are concerned with the consolidation of their positions (that is, the personalisation of their authority).

They systematically mutilate and distort their various constitutions, suspending them where expedient and making them appear to be not more than working papers. A constitution amendable twice or thrice a year merely because the President wants things at his convenience is nothing more than his personal diary. They set up and perpetuate one party dictatorships and make democracy as scarce as a dog's tears. The masses are manipulated, cheated out of every imaginable right, dehumanized with infused hypocrisy, and mercilessly exploited. Yet this very populace is presented to foreign aiders as miserable 'primitive' victims of natural hazards for whom songs must be sung, races against time organised the world over, bread baked, woollen blankets made, and drugs sent in iron boxes labelled: "We give to conquer". If only these leaders could be honest enough with themselves to see that the real disasters, the preponderant hazards in

Africa are manmade and political, not natural!

As concerns the distribution of power, the African Heads of State are neither modern nor traditional. In the traditional African states, there was and still is (where these have been allowed to persist) devolution of power and authority. The king had his lords, notables and village heads who equally wielded power. The very fear and respect he had for the ancestors guaranteed the devolution of power and authority. In the Western Grassfields of Cameroon for example, the Fon must not decide single handedly or act whimsically. He has to decide and act concertedly with his Kwifon (Kwifo' or Nwarong), which is a sort of council comprising all his regional representatives and advisers. The Kwifon is sometimes referred to as 'The Voice Of The People'. And I dare say the people have a genuine reason for doing so, for each of the Grassfield kingdoms has effectively institutionalised checks against the abuse of power by the king. This is because their constitution which is sacred is kept under the custody of the ancestors. The king can't have access to it any time he dreams or fantasizes.

But what do we notice in the modern African states? First, the Heads of State destroy the ladders that were indispensable in their climbs into supremacy. Second, they accumulate functions: Head of State, Head of Government, Head of Party, Supreme Commander of the forces (some of them cannot operate a mere rifle), Chairman of the Supreme Court of Justice, Grand Chancellor, Minister of Defense and Finance (strategic, these), and what have you. Furthermore, they choose as collaborators only men that sleep at cabinet meetings, sign documents without reading over, are treacherous to their families and friends, collaborators whose only diplomatic excellence is the unfailing ability to say "Yes, D'accord, C'est ça" and who send His Excellency good will messages all the year long, and to his wife, the latest gifts for sale in Europe, America or the Soviet Union.

Finally, when their dictatorships have been fully established, these Heads of State invite their fellow countrymen to invent songs, forge poems, write books and build monuments, all in praise of them and their caprices. Their media and journalists are there to promote their good name and must always play down their Western critics who deplore their notorious habits and irritating extravagance. Give me a different definition of a demi-god if you can!

I write this article because many people tend to compare today's African Heads of State with the traditional ruler. There is little or no similarity between these two. Even as concerns the singing of praises, the praise-singers of today are not like those of old. Today, people are either compelled to sing praises, or they do so hypocritically in order to win favours for themselves. Whereas in the traditional states, praise singing was (and to a limited extent still is) spontaneous and cultural. One poet has aptly described the barrenness and disrespectability of today's praise-singer, in the following unequivocal terms:

"The public praise-singer," he writes, "like the firm fruitless fig tree, to defy the just mouth of Age, must shed his intangible words and revise his song styles to feed the whims of Seasons with an absurd assembly of songs, as more Masters make a name and go."

African Heads of State today, are therefore neither modern nor traditional in the Weberian sense of these words. Where to class the African Heads of State remains the question. A serious question, for Weber is no longer there to provide us with a third category. Do you have an answer?

Dr B has a good sense of humour. See the captivating manner in which he ends the article. I'm sure the space provided him in the review was quite small; his examples and allusions have definitely been suppressed.

For I know him as one who loves facts. Like myself, he hates the idea of people being confused between their personal opinions and what is real and objectively perceptible. His article is as lucid and factual as my poem on Bastos and Briqueterie; I congratulate him on that. He is the type of person who would like to have all philosophy books burnt, and philosophers taught the rigorous techniques of fieldwork. He would admit philosophers are intellectuals alright, but who have a weakness in that they lack the time to visit archives and the courage to come face to face with their society; they would rather migrate to Heaven or to Hell in order to investigate the world, just like running away from one's object of study.

If the Honourable V.M shows any appreciation for this particular gift, then he will have many more in future. Perhaps my gift is belated. For how do I expect the Honourable V.M not to have read the political article in the famous IRAP? And why would the government ban what they themselves haven't read? I don't want to believe that the authorities depend on hearsay as well, just like the rest of us. I believe the Boss should encourage them at least to read political journals, provided of course he himself is interested in reading. For nobody readily encourages interest where he is disinterested, except when doing that would favour him somehow. But why should a President possibly lack interest in the culture of the intellect? It could be that he is barely literate and can hardly read fluently nor understand easily. Or it could be that he has nothing to learn from political journals, perhaps simply because he needs no more political weapon than his potent amulets and charms to resolve the complex conflicts inherent in modern leadership.

Somehow I feel that Dr B's prolific critical writings make the President reluctant to assimilate him into the system. It doesn't usually take the President this long to determine whether or not to silence a critic with a sizeable piece of the national cake. Just as it takes a dissembler to silence another, it takes an intellectual to accept another. Moreover, there is every reason to fear that once in Dr B would see far more to write about than he does at present. For he is very unlike the pseudo-intellectuals who would cease to criticise as soon as they've got their share of the national cake. He might realise that everybody in the cabinet is blind to the 'rising expectations' of the masses and too keen on self-aggrandizement and foreign banking. He might realise that the greatest worry of everyone in this privileged group is how to devise and maintain a permanent signature, because in Swiss banks they have all, at one time or another, had urgent emergency services delayed because their signatures had slight variations. They hate to stay in Switzerland for long, lest they arouse suspicion back home. And how they must hate those foreign News Agencies which seize the slightest opportunity to publicize private visits, thus scandalising African leaders!

Yes, Dr B is a radical danger. I believe he would be languishing at the BMM today, if he hadn't a worldwide reputation. He can write anything at any time, and no one would dare to ask him any question. The most the government can do is ban the circulation of all journals containing his writings. But the authorities aren't always successful in doing this, for the more people know that a piece of writing is banned, the greater their craving to read the underground copies of it! Everybody listens whenever Dr B speaks, whether they like it or not. It is alleged that once he wrote an essay that was so critical of the government and so embarrassing to some of its Western allies that the president invited him for questioning.

Dr B went to the presidency in shirt sleeves and was stopped by the guards from getting in. When later on the President telephoned to find out why on earth he had turned down a presidential invitation, Dr B said: "It needs more than just a presidential invitation to see the President; an invitation by the guards is even more important!" When he went again, the President was there in person at the gate to receive him! Yet Dr. B. was still in shirt sleeves! I believe after the meeting he wrote down somewhere 'no suit, no President', to remind himself of the confrontation with Le Père Jean Mouton some years back. However, it is said that he asked the President if he had found as much as a comma out of place. "Show me, and I will rectify it," he is said to have added. Others would wonder how he dared to speak like that to the President. But I think that when your conscience is clear, and when your genuine intention is to bring about betterment for all and sundry, even vicious tyrants are afraid to do something to hurt you. One only thinks of hurting someone one knows one can hurt in the first place. No hunter goes out of his way to attack a tiger when he isn't convinced he would get the better of it.

That said, one must admit that Genuine Intellectuals are a fine lot! So self-confident! And justifiably so. Hearsay holds it that the Department of Sociology had become so radically subversive that the government decidedly closed it down. But Dr B was so furious with the contemptible authorities that the President almost sent him a handwritten apology. I like Dr B's assertiveness. If our ministers and vice-ministers could be only half as assertive, our country would have gone a long way towards ceasing to be a Third World nation. But if the present order of things persists, we are most likely to lose grip of everything that facilitates a positive march forward.

It's strange how crowded my thoughts are! I can't think of a thing without thinking of another! What a mental curse! May God help me out of such a mess. Didn't I start by blaming the Honourable V.M for criticising me over much? Then why did I abandon that train of thought? Why did I delve into Dr B's article? Was it timely and appropriate or was it forced? That I can't say, but I fear I have a defective mind! Concentration is what I badly need. For truly a man is no good who cannot concentrate. The story is told in my village of a husband who always ate kolanuts at the same time as he made love to his wife. But when his first two children were both very weak (all kola and no nuts, the villagers would say), he made up his mind to be fully committed thence; and I dare say things changed! So no more flirtatious thinking. Back to my deserted flock I go. Yes, 'flock' I mean. I'm no leader now, but who says I won't be?

I'm still waiting for the divine command, am I not? Yes, I'm still waiting, because I've refused to take my dream at the Honourable V.M's residence for the long awaited signal from above.

Why did the Honourable V.M express such surprise when I told him I have one Advanced Level G.C.E paper? He blamed me that I am deliberately inviting misery upon myself in order to say that the country is bad and that its leaders are corrupt and irresponsible. But I totally disagreed with him, though I dared not tell him that. At least there is one thing I have that nobody can deprive me of, as long as I live. That thing is my freedom of thought. No government, no matter how coercive, can subdue my thoughts.

The Honourable V.M seems to look at the country through the rose coloured glasses of his office and residence; in short his social status. He speaks and acts like a tape recording which can't be held responsible for what comes out of it. What does he think is an Advanced level paper? Does he value it so much because he hasn't one himself? Maybe. But there is a reality he grossly ignores. He isn't aware of the unpleasant fact that there are over 10,000 jobless degree holders in the country at the moment. He doesn't know that if I'm interested in a job at this stage, it is mainly because I failed to obtain the number of Advanced level papers necessary for me to seek admission into the National University.

How I love to study in the Faculty of Arts and Social Thought. Since the confrontation I witnessed between Le Père Jean Mouton and Dr B a long time ago, I have always loved sociology. That is why I've read a lot of books in this domain ever since. Perhaps one day I shall discover that I'm a sociologist without a qualification. God bless that day! I shall offer a special mass, and Dr B shall be present to do the first reading!

I've been thinking of Dr Q too. What an admirable chap! How many Cameroonians like him would readily accept to be undervalued academically, in the name of nation-building. How many are ready to see as he did, that the PhD cannot make the man? A PhD is not there to shout "Open Sesame," to the hurdles of development, nor is it there to serve as a magic wand. The false and blind belief in the magical power of certificates is the root cause of the Third World disease called Diplomania; a disease which like most others, has its highest incidence in the Dark Continent. In Europe the importance people give to academic qualifications isn't as general as in the Third World; rather, it varies from country to country. In Germany for instance, people are said to love titles so much that the wife of a university professor would boycott a shop if the shopkeeper forgets to address her "Mrs professor", or "Mrs Prof. Dr Dr", depending on the number of PhD her husband has. I personally think that Diplomania is a bad disease that needs immediate eradication. The sooner a vaccine is developed for it, the better. If this is not done, we will soon have people with the PhD who cannot spell their names correctly or those of their specialties.

I hear that academically Cameroon is a force to reckon with in Africa, despite all the perceptible shortcomings of its educational system. "Let's not contribute towards any conscious or unconscious attempt to weaken this image," one of our diplomaniacs is likely to shout out. I say to hell with him! I've also heard whispers here and there that the system of professional education left behind by the French is to be revised and somewhat reconciled with the main academic trunk, the National University. From what Dr Q said, those of them with purely academic qualifications don't seem to like in the least the great disparity in salaries between themselves and the "trained" administrators or "integrated professionals" as they are proudly referred to by the perpetrators of mediocrity. The reason the graduates complain so bitterly is that they believe these "integrated professionals" have no greater expertise in their supposed fields of excellence than any novice. This might be a mere presumption, but at the moment I'm incapable of taking sides. Not being a civil servant myself, I know next to nothing about salaries.

But I'm happy I'm going to start work next week. I must prepare seriously for it. I have never worked in an office before. Completely strange for one in a country where reigns supra-bureaucracy, isn't it? Until now I have worked as houseboy and as teacher of English to Francophone families. Both have been interesting jobs, and my experiences have been very enriching. I remember a pathetic incident when my wages as houseboy were withheld because I dared to eat the leftovers of the delicious meal I had prepared and served my master and his family. I lost my latest job as teacher of English for a different reason.

I was employed to teach English to an ambitious couple, who wanted to gain social prominence through a mastery of the two official languages. At that time, there was a lot of noise going on amongst the Francophones about the political expediency of knowing some English. Noise motivated by a sad episode that befell the President's minister of commerce on an official visit with him to the US. The minister in question had replied by giving his name when asked by his American counterpart: "How do you do?". Angry with his minister for making a fool of his glorious idea of a bilingual cabinet, the President who himself could boast he was bilingual because he spoke French and some amount of Pidgin English, dismissed the minister. The President's claim to bilingualism was false, but he was in charge, which made all the difference. My employers didn't think that to speak and understand Pidgin English was enough for them to claim knowledge of English. And that is why I taught them impeccable Shakespearean English as spoken in England today.

This couple had a big supermarket at the commercial centre, where each of them had to oversee the sales for some days of the week. So when the wife was at the shop, I taught the husband, and vice versa. At first things went so smoothly that I almost thought my job a permanent one. As a business couple my employers offered a lot of parties at their residence uphill in Bastos. They were also very mobile, constantly oscillating between the great city and the even greater city of Paris. All this meant that I had to forgo giving some lectures despite myself, and for which I was never remunerated. The final blow came when my master unexpectedly returned home one day to find me acting sentinel to his wife who was love-making in their conjugal bed with a handsome university student. Despite all I said to wash my hands of the matter, I was still dismissed; the guilty wife stayed on after a few unconvincing words of apology. It was a conspiracy to fire me, yes, a conspiracy to fire me because they were jealous of my abilities. For one thing, I had a perfect command of English; they didn't, and must have felt bad. I always thought they did, and the fact that they fired me when I wasn't at fault, confirmed this.

I have heard that employers set many such mean traps when they are tired of an employee. Some even arrange with their wives who pretend to seduce the worker in question. The master then comes in time to surprise them fondling. The poor lad is then fired, and most often is never paid the salary of the past five months. Some naively count themselves lucky not to have been sent to prison. As far as I am concerned, nobody with any sense of dignity would allow a university student to make love to his wife simply because he wants to fire a voiceless wretch. It's a pity that my employers weren't as sophisticated as they appeared! Looks can be so deceitful!

All the above meanness remind me of yet another. I have a neighbour at Briqueterie who is far more of a wretch than myself. He is called Stephen Asabi, and is married to a barren young beauty. Both of them come from Akonolinga and have nothing doing, yet they have survived famine for the past seven years that I know them. But there is a secret about it all. Mr. Stephen Asabi is obliged to make love to his wife during the day, because at night she has to go out ahunting for money. There is no nightclub, no matter how sophisticated or vulgar, which this barren beauty doesn't visit. She spends the whole night out and returns in the morning ready to feed Mr Stephen Asabi and herself. Many a time I have turned down her invitation for a meal with them. I would rather be starved to death!

Sometimes I'm forced to think that this woman would carry home a bundle of disaster one day. Nobody can safely do such a business all her life. Perhaps she is responsible for her husband's sickness. Oh! how I wonder that a man can be so pale, yet live! He barely has the energy to crawl out of his hut and sit in front of their room, where he spends time attacking the flies attracted to the sores on his face, arms and feet. How such an ugly man should have a beautiful though barren woman like her! Perhaps it's she who has ruined his life, destroyed his charm and infected his good looks. It's a pity, isn't it?

Yes, perhaps she has infected him with all the venereal diseases that plague this society. Those sores of his make me think of syphilis, yes, syphilis. He has syphilis, I think; that is why I'm scared of them, scared of eating with them. One must not take chances; living in Briqueterie is miserable enough in itself! So I endeavour to stay away from the women, the corrupting prostitutes, I mean.

Prostitution, I know so much about it, especially about prostitution in Europe, its place of birth. Through hearsay, I've learnt that it is one of the most well developed industries anywhere in Europe. Concerned with earning money through tourism, European countries have left no stone unturned in promoting prostitution. They've worked so hard, and successfully too, that today their governments can afford to provide for everybody the barest minimum to survive. Some countries have acknowledged the great contribution made to their economies by prostitution; they have erected monuments dedicated to the leading prostitutes of their time. That's what I call success, real success!

I've read that visiting prostitutes is a very systematic affair amongst international businessmen, holiday makers, foreign students and diplomatic delegations or missions. African Presidents and their ministers have been known to be influenced by the level of hospitality of prostitutes to prefer visiting one Western country to another. Flagrant cases have been registered of some such leaders who chose to stay underdeveloped, rather than be helped out of the mess by a Developed country with a record for racist prostitutes.

Visiting prostitutes is a procedural affair. A man arrives in a city, cleans himself up and puts on his best attire, and examines himself in front of a big mirror and under a red light. He then goes out to the nearest brothel. He rings the door bell and is allowed in. The manager presents him with photographs of the various women under him. These women are many and carefully selected to satisfy men of every possible taste. (Tastes among African leaders and businessmen are said to be "shaped by this or that actress, which I saw in this or that blue movie". They all go for what they've internalised way back home in Africa – the blondes, so it is rumoured.) The visitor selects the one who pleases him and is indicated her room but is allowed to start no operation before payment.

The story is told of an African President who dismissed his foreign minister because they both happened to have visited the same brothel and to have chosen the same blonde when on an official visit in a European country renowned for its beautiful prostitutes. But I personally don't see why the President had to be so hard on his minister, taken as true the rumour that the latter owed his ministerial post to the fact that he had agreed to allow the President to do with his wife what the president pleased. The President should have judged well that a man has to need a post very much if he is ready to sacrifice his wife for it. Generally, Africa has the politics of "one good turn deserves another". Things are so unstable and coup d'états so rampant that one's subordinate today can be one's superior tomorrow. Perhaps this explains why killing is so fashionable in the African political arena.

I'm now convinced that whites will never stop thinking of themselves as superior to blacks, not even prostitutes! Imagine what I heard a French prostitute did to a young Cameroonian student! This student went to Lyon to polish up his French in order to satisfy the bilingual options of the government. While there he felt like to visit a prostitute, and did just that. But what happened! This young white delinquent would not have anything to do with my countryman unless he allowed his penis to be washed for 30 minutes with a strong medicated soap. I personally congratulate the young man for disallowing such nonsense!

All this prostitute had to do was declare herself a racist prostitute and allow my countryman to venture elsewhere for another with interracial sentiments. I advise that no African should ever allow his personality and dignity to be trampled upon by every nitwit or nonentity of the white race. Hit back, and hit back hard, should be our guiding principle. How I wish I were in Europe to personally teach them a lesson!

I have a reason for always avoiding to think of prostitution in my country. Prostitution in Cameroon is so mean, dirty and confused. A state of affairs which is reflected in the vocabulary used to denote the practice; there are a thousand and one gutter words and phrases used to denote the revolting practice – words which make one feel sick. I hate to think of this gutter vocabulary, because I don't want to feel sick at this time of day. However, prostitution in Cameroon is mean because I've heard that politicians use prostitutes to stifle their opponents. Young succulent women have been used by highly placed politicians to poison men who would have contributed ably towards solving Cameroon's present political and economic mediocrity. Some pseudo-intellectuals have been poisoned by the dangerous beehives that lie in a woman's lap, while others have simply been shocked to death by the current that lies beneath the apparent apples on her chest. The saddest case I came to know of, through hearsay as usual, is that of a prominent opponent whose wife applied a poisonous lipstick, then kissed him to death. A crime for which she was rewarded both in cash and in kind by the President.

Prostitution is Cameroon is dirty because many women are forced into it by circumstances. Quite unlike in Europe where a girl might grow up and deliberately choose upon prostitution as the best way to spend her sex and professional life, so I hear. At that level, the European prostitute should be proud of her profession which she is ready to defend anytime anywhere. Perhaps that explains why a French free girl can afford to lose money for such a silly reason as that "un nègre" refused to have his "penis washed for 30 minutes with a strong medicated soap". The situation in Cameroon is different. How many Cameroonian prostitutes can afford "a strong medicated soap" even for their own use? Not as many as one in ten! No exaggeration about it at all.

Yes, circumstances force Cameroonians to prostitute. Economic, social and political misery force young girls and women into prostitution. What do we expect from a young girl who suddenly realises that she lacks the money to live up to the standards that modernity has defined for her? What do we expect from a young girl who is shocked to realise that young men prefer 'kick and go' relationships to lasting ones? How do we expect a jobless divorced woman to live, even averagely? What do we expect from young girls who cannot be admitted into the National University because the policy of regional balances requires that only this or that number of students from this or that ethnic group be given a place each year? And so on and so forth.

Prostitution is also confused because it is hard to distinguish between a prostitute and a non-prostitute. There is no sense of professionalism; everything is muddled. Let's take as professionals those free women who live on their own, and who do nothing else for livelihood but unproductive love making. That is good enough. But let's again take ourselves into any of the nightclubs, or to any other hotspot in town. What do we realise? A real strange and dramatic turning of the tables! We remark that those who dart about here and there urging and scheming to be taken home by any man with a fat wallet are not the said professionals! They are those who during the day denounce and deny to have anything to do with prostitution. They are those who would take you to court just for talking openly about prostitution. They are the university girls, the secondary and high school students, and the spinsters who are dissatisfied with what they earn as civil servants. They are also the miserable housewives like the wife of Mr. Stephen Asabi. They invade the field and make those who entirely depend on it for livelihood even more miserable. The added effect of all this infringement is that women rapidly lose respect and appear very cheap to the men, who know that all they need do to have one is be ready to dispense with a bottle of beer, a packet of cigarettes, or some sticks of "Soya beef".

It is a real pathetic situation. That is why I always try to avoid thinking of it. Let's even consider the incidence of V.D in our towns. V.D which I'm told the 'Born Again' Christians have nicknamed 'V.D.A', meaning 'Vicious Danger in the Abyss'. Whatever they mean! However, what we would remark is that two out of every three school girls are reported to harbour at least one disease of Amour; diseases passed on to them mostly by responsible people, sophisticated people in big offices. While the supposed professionals are not so rotten yet. This indicates that the intruders have not only usurped their clients, but have also relieved them of their pathological burdens.

Lord God, kindly sprinkle some of your grace upon the women of my country. Make them strive to solve their problems in morally upright ways despite the mountain of obstacles they face. Make them understand that suffering makes life worth living; also make the authorities see that there is a difference between this necessary suffering and imposed misery. I ask thee through Christ my saviour. Amen. I know it is my place as God's chosen messenger to take care of the world, to pray and wish for a better state of affairs. I should demonstrate my leadership qualities, by showing concern as I do, so God might not feel disappointed in me.

How will office life be like? Sitting everyday behind a table, will I be able? I will do my best to keep this particular job longest. It is an offer by the government; my own share of the national cake. Would it suffice for someone with an appetite like mine? Perhaps working with the government is the beginning of all. Shall the day come when I will also stride confidently along the corridors of political power? Time will tell. Though somehow I fear the adverse effects of regional and ethnic planification and balanced development. Since everyone in office in Cameroon is appointed so that he might stake out a portion of the national cake both for himself and his region, I can understand the controversy the appointment of someone like myself would bring about.

My country's political philosophy has no place for Cameroonians who, like myself, happen to be everywhere and nowhere in particular! We've been made the victims of a mess we didn't help bring about. A mess because of which I've become a disfavoured Cameroonian with stifled political ambitions! One with no regional attachments, thus without a power base! I can't contribute towards national development, not because I don't want to, but because the political philosophy in practice excludes people of my kind and background. What a curse!

PART FIVE

It is strange how fast time passes. Who would believe that I've been a civil servant for three years already? What wonderful changes have taken place, changes both internal and external to me! I was brought in, I became a student, and I'm now an integral part of the system. And I don't see how I can possibly cease to belong to it. As a system it is good to those of its elements who coordinate its veritable reins. At that level it is a sweet system, sweet as ripe banana fruit. I remember what my blind and helpless grandfather used to tell me as an infant, that he had acquired his first ever pair of shorts and shirt from an old white man to whom he had offered a bunch of stolen bananas. I regret to add that he further damaged his eyes when he also took upon himself to use the powerful glasses his old white man forgot in his place. Ah! God bless my pleasant discovery!

For three years I've seen what it means to be a top civil servant. Nothing is as good as working as the Private Secretary of an Honourable V.M. Haven't I become used to monthly tips that greatly surpass my salary? Haven't I attended many an important conference? Is there any state secret I do not know? Can I remember when I last bought food, beer or whisky with my own money?

Don't I just need to come home from a cocktail party, a party meeting or a seminar with whatever amount of food and drinks I want? What stationery do I lack? In which business and political circles am I not known? And as proof of all these changes, those who knew me when misery was my closest companion have had to revise their mental representations of me. Instead of the dull-faced young man flat as a thin leaf, I am now a bustling epicurean with a large stomach that reminds me of good living. I love it!

I've seen things, strange things, really marvellous things. The Honourable V.M actually has every reason to continue his nocturnal visits to Briqueterie. All is worth the struggle. Life in Cameroon isn't the apparent daily version common to everybody; the real life is much more covert and interesting. Major decisions are taken in a hurry over the telephone, at cocktail parties, in conference centres, on the hotel corridors, and at snack bars and chicken parlours. It isn't by the force of official duties well executed that civil servants are promoted; rather, it is in all sorts of out-of-office milieus that they campaign for positions. Civil servants know that when it actually comes to working their way up, their immediate bosses don't count for much; they look beyond him, to those higher up the hierarchy. So no one really cares to do his or her work properly, because they know that whatever form of punishment their immediate bosses propose, if ever they are foolish enough to, or if they have that much time to waste, would be cancelled by their superiors. And so is the spiral of cancellations; it goes up and up, until it disappears into the presidency. Everyone campaigns for promotion. Even the 'chef de table' and 'chef de table adjoint' in the various offices have to campaign vigorously; it makes all the difference between two occupants of an office table, when the one is the chief of table and the other is the deputy chief of table.

My country is a place for the rich, the very rich. One and half years ago the Honourable V.M had a land dispute with a young wretch back in his home town. Everyone knew that it was a case the Honourable V.M could never win. But he smiled and I smiled also. We knew our way around the place. The telephone rang twice or thrice, and the tables were turned. And no folk understood how the magistrate had perceived the case and applied the law that the Honourable V.M should come out victorious. The poor shouldn't venture into our circles because they can't cope. Why not cut one's coat according to one's cloth?

And talking about coats, I remarked a strange thing of late. The Honourable V.M was about to leave for Europe to attend a meeting. One of his immediate subordinates, a Director at the Vice-Ministry, telephoned in his absence. I promised to deliver the message to him on his return. The Director had telephoned to tell the Honourable V.M of a new suit he bought for the latter in view of the European trip. Ask why a suit should be presented to one who has three giant wardrobes full of them, or why a gift at all, and you are the naive citizen I was three years ago. For in Cameroon, junior civil servants present gifts of all sorts to their superiors, in order to enhance their chances of being promoted. It is from little beginnings – that is, through bribes sprinkled here and there, now and again – that great progress is made in the system. They are simply countless, the opportunities one has in our society to become richer and more socially visible!

It is good to know. I'm pleased to know. So I finally registered in the National University, not in the Department of Sociology as was for long my dream, but in the Department of Rhetoric and Laws. The Honourable V.M discouraged me about sociology, and I saw his point. I now understand why Dr B has never been and might never be made minister. Such people as he and Dr Q are no use for the country. They claim to know much and for this reason they think it's their right to criticise and subvert our institutions. I hear from reliable superiors that the Department will soon be banned for good if Dr B continues to criticise the government with his characteristic arrogance. Our Great Comrade the President, having fortified himself with more potent amulets and charms specially prepared for him by the greatest witchdoctor in the land, is ready to face up to the notorious Dr B this time! But since there is no one to warn Dr B, he will surely continue to criticise, and the Great Comrade is sure to strike like lightning. I doubt if Dr B would listen to any advice at all. He is like a foil to his own life. Can't he see that life is too sweet and too short to be wasted arguing over trifles?

In the Department of Rhetoric and Laws things are easy for persons like me. I'm very friendly with all my lecturers. They give me copies of their pamphlets, as well as possible examination questions. I invite them out to chicken parlours and snack bars, and provide them with inside information. We actually are very fond of one another. I supply them with all the stationery they need to produce their expensive pamphlets. I help them photocopy chunks of pages from textbooks, which they sell to the students. Above all, I take care of their interests in the public service and provide them with information on their promotion prospects, so they know exactly when they are falling in or out of favour with the administration. They've been most helpful too. I've led my class since I registered. In a year or two I'm sure to graduate with a "Licence". I see prospects everywhere. Hundreds of students never make their examinations. But that's because they believe they can make it entirely on their own. I couldn't care less about students who refuse to understand the society in which they live. Everyone for himself and God for us all.

Without the Honourable V.M's intervention, I wouldn't have been admitted at the university with one advanced level paper only. But "Rhetoric and Laws" are what the country needs, and particularly from faithful citizens that it can trust. Don't we make the 'texte de base' of the university? Aren't these laws made and unmade by us? So don't argue any further, Monsieur le Doyen. And remember to see me tomorrow at 4.30 p.m. as we've agreed." That is what the Honourable V.M told the Dean of the Faculty. The next day they shared a bottle of champagne together and discussed their common interests in detail, promising mutual support. And so I became admitted. Now I lead the class, while those who had the required qualification are incapable of making a basic pass! I hope my example will teach the academic community a reality they seem to have ignored: That the Advanced Level Examination isn't the true test of knowledge.

The recent Baccalauréat scandal made enemies of the Republic wrongly rejoice that they had got the Minister of State for Education and Superior Endeavours at last. He was alleged to have altered the results, so many people with a utopic idea of democracy thought that our Great Comrade would dismiss him. But to have thought such a thing is to have exhibited gross ignorance of the realities of the country. The sort of ignorance that I was guilty of three years ago. But I'm purged of that, and thank God it didn't happen a minute too late!

First and foremost, is a minister automatically dismissed merely because he manipulates the Baccalauréat examination results, so that his daughter who never sat for it could make an excellent pass? Moreover, the minister had even twice postponed the said examination, each time with the hope that his daughter might get well in time to write it. But with his high sense of patriotism, rather than continue to immobilize the whole country because of his sick daughter, he preferred to put the state machinery at work. It was easy to make his daughter gain the best Baccalauréat results. After all, she was very intelligent, and had proven this all her scholarly years. In fact, those who criticize the minister do so blindly. Which is a more responsible thing to do: let the examination go ahead and give the daughter a pass, or prolong it until the sick daughter gets well? Moreover, why can't those who criticise take time to look through the girl's progress record? They would remark that her academic profile actually reflects the daughter of the Minister of State for Education and Superior Endeavours that she is: Ever leading her class!

However, the minister wasn't dismissed as many had wished. I say bravo to our Great Comrade. He should always avoid being swayed by ruinous public opinion; it is a bitter drug that needs to be taken with a salted glass of water always. The minister maintained his portfolio for obvious reasons. First because the Great Comrade is boss and would rightly not tolerate being dictated by ignorant people who can't even boast of the basics of good government. Second, he would not dismiss for so trivial a reason the son of a Lamido he respects very much. Nobody who cares for his life and position would like to be cursed by the ancestors. The Lamido represents the ancestors here on earth; he represents the Great Comrade's very own late father! And he knows he cannot spit on the Minister's face without making the Lamido angry and consequently his late father. Africans know that the parent who respects tradition will live long enough to see his children develop grey hair. Third, I consider the Great Comrade a person who thinks things over before making a decision. He is very foresighted. He knows that his daughter is in the School of Medicines, and that one day she will have to write her final examination. It could also happen that she falls sick just before the said examination. And if she can't get well in time, would he ruin her medical career simply because she fell sick during examination? No, never! She is a very intelligent girl, even more intelligent than the daughter of the Minister of State for Education and Superior Endeavours. So it would be legitimate for her to top her class with a "Mention Très Honourable avec Felicitation du Jury", or a "Mention Incroyable avec Felicitation des Camarades de Classe". That is realism, pragmatism is what I mean; the thing we need more than any other in Cameroon. May Allah be with us in all our designs. Amen.

I have evacuated Briqueterie and moved uphill to Nlongkak which is closest to Bastos. Since I acquired a second hand car from Belgium, it became imperative to change quarters. At Briqueterie there's scarcely a house with a garage, because the houses are so crammed together. But that's alright for the people who live there, isn't it? For all I know, one can't own a car and still live at Briqueterie. Where I'm at present is both geographically and materially midway between Briqueterie and Bastos, because we daily aspire to live like the residents of the latter quarters. What we the aspirants need is a little encouragement and support, enhancing promotions in the civil service to accomplish our climb.

A sudden change of class entails a whole change in one's personality. And I have had to reckon with many social attributes that necessarily follow one up this ambitious ladder. There has been a primary change at the level of appearance, which has to reflect my class. I have had to make new friends who befit my status, friends with whom I have everything in common. I also eat three times a day, no more no less. And the rhythm of my meals is in tune with the meal times of our patrons at Bastos, who in turn listen keenly to bells that chime from across the Atlantic Ocean. So I cook when they cook, and eat when they eat. I go jogging on Sundays to keep fit just as they do. Even my sleeping times are regulated by theirs.

More and more I've felt the need for a companion. So some weeks ago I looked for a beautiful university girl. This girl now lives with me and helps in the cooking. I'm observing her keenly. My previous girlfriend was rather a naive high school girl, who became pregnant the very first time we made love. I was quite irritated by her naivety and took her straightaway to a medical student who is a good friend of mine, and a specialist in abortions that aren't exactly legal. It didn't take him half an hour to terminate the pregnancy for which I gave him a handsome reward. Then I paid the girl off. I hope that this one is different. I think she is, even if for no other reason but the fact that she is a university student. To succeed in this our beautiful country, one must be very, very realistic. To hell with those so-called intellectuals who try to look beyond their noses! Or who are always weeping more than the owners of a corpse! Who tells them that 'the Masses' are so desperate that they want help from them? I think that we in authority ought to teach them a lesson they will never forget! I will discuss this particular issue with the Honourable V.M, my mentor.

I have a feeling that the critics of our government are financed from abroad. Because I cannot understand why they can't bring themselves to see things the way every other person does. Why their incessant attempt to view from another perspective? Always fishing for trouble. How insatiable they are! They may continue, but I would like to inform them that they sign their own death warrants without knowing. Every criticism they make takes them nearer their graves, because we are not going to forgive or forget their wrong doings! I dislike the so-called 'Genuine Intellectuals' most of all: Those men and women who poke their noses into issues that have nothing in common with the disciplines that made them obsessed with academic titles. They should rather spend time treating their sick books and leave politics and public related issues to those of us who know what these things are all about. They claim that the Government is vicious. I understand why. They have failed to make a headway into it. I know 'The Fox and The Sour Grapes' story just too well. So they resort to making slanderous statements and to writing subversive tracts. Could it be that the BMM's are too full for more prisoners? If not, what could the diehard critics of our institutions be taking advantage of? What is behind the recent upsurge of antigovernment propaganda, that worries me so much? Whatever is responsible, it won't be long before that crack on the wall is mended. But if this can be explained by the fact that the BMM's are too full, all I need to tell the subversives is: "Be patient my lords, your turn is coming". The BMM's will soon be cleared, then they can get in. In addition, the Great Comrade has just commissioned the building of a new prison in the home village of one of his closest collaborators, as a reward for his unflinching loyalty and support!

Meanwhile I would these intellectuals spend their lives usefully. Life is too sweet and too short to be wasted on petty matters of ideology and principle. There is much of sociological value for Dr B to study outside the domain of politics. For instance, it is in no way subversive to make a study of secret societies such as Fâmlà and religious sects like the various 'Born Again' movements, as long as he doesn't suggest that political, social and economic frustrations are responsible for their proliferation. That is what we don't want to hear; that is subversion, and we won't tolerate it. What I would like him and others of his kind to study is to describe in a simple and straightforward manner, with no insinuations whatsoever, the phenomena of secret societies and sects in Cameroon. Done in that way, with no biting criticism of those in power or of the system in place, such studies are sure to be distributed in schools for students' use; the authors themselves would be given something to live on by the government. That is what I call being alert, being pragmatic!

Two days ago a big businessman who is noted for printing false banknotes approached me after work. He was sweating profusely, and fright was written all over his face. I asked him what the problem was. He told me that he was being pursued by spirits. I didn't understand, so he went right ahead to explain. He belonged to a secret society of the ten biggest businessmen in the country. This group is called Fâmlà Bami, and its members can be as rich as they want to be, if and only if they fulfill one preponderant condition. They must each sacrifice twelve people every year; one person per month. He found it difficult to fulfil that promise. So he ran away from the group when he bought his money-making machine. But a week ago the spirits threatened him again with a note stating: "You either settle your debt in a month, or you lose your life." Where would he get twelve people to sacrifice in a month? That is what he had come to ask me, so that I could tell him of a competent marabout who could chase away the spirits once and for all. So I sent him to the best witchdoctor I know in

Briqueterie. But at a fee, of course. Nothing goes for nothing. In the civil service you can't be rich fast enough if you ignore such little tips for services rendered.

That is the type of thing I would like the intellectuals to study. Examples abound of Fâmlà and similar secret societies. There is the story of a student who, after failing to make a pass in the Baccalauréat for five consecutive years, joined a Fâmlà society. There he started sacrificing his relatives in order to be rich. When this became a scandal, the few remaining relatives called him to talk to him. But he failed to listen. He reiterated that he wanted money, any money. "L'argent c'est l'argent, Fâmlà ou non," he insisted. Thus the intellectuals should get themselves involved in real scientific studies. They should explore the world of sorcery and make academic capital out of it. Such are examples of what I term innocent scientific studies that would hurt no one. Instead, they would provide the researcher with his daily bread, in this difficult world of ours. But if the intellectuals fail to heed my advice, and prefer to play about with hot coal, that's their funeral. They should remember that the devil has work for idle hands. Let those who have ears hear; only the fly with no one to advise it is likely to accompany the corpse into the grave.

Many people are surprised that the Honourable V.M should now like me so much. All I dare say is that they will continue to be surprised. My climb is just beginning. Perhaps they would pretend not to have heard the people's saying that a goat eats where it is tethered. I'm eating up the ladder where the Almighty God has placed me. Yes, just that. It is all planned out in Heaven; as in Heaven, so on Earth. All I do here on Earth is execute divine orders. Mine is a divine mission, of which I'm just too aware. May the Lord be praised.

✫ ✫ ✫

I would have been angry if Rev. Father Limbo had not accepted my proposal without modification. It is all scheduled for next Sunday. The mass will be a thanksgiving one, offered by me for me. The Honourable V.M is a man of foresight. He initiated it all, then asked me to think over it. I still recall his words: "You must always thank the Lord for all the good things that come your way. He is the light of the world; the maker and unmaker of all kings!" Yes, everything has been organised. Everyone knows that there is a party after mass. The Honourable V.M is very willing to allow me use his hall. He has even subsidised my financial efforts.

Dr T, Mrs S, and Prof. N have also given some financial support. They all love me very much. Since I began to climb, they have increasingly integrated me into their circle. I now have a permanent front seat in the church and take part in the readings. None of the other members of the congregation seems to find anything to criticise about this. It appears that each and every one of them has always believed that is the way things should go; that is to say, that the big and the rich be given privileged treatment. Which I think is perfectly normal, given our onerous duties and commitments.

I know what next Sunday has in store for me. I honestly pray that everything should turn out as planned. It will perhaps mark a great turning point, whence I will start listening to the radio on Saturdays and Sundays. It even appears the Honourable V.M has covertly chosen me as his most likely successor in the administration, after successfully arranging a change of tribe of birth and origin for me. The supporting documents are carefully locked away in my briefcase, while some copies have been slipped into my files at the Ministry of Public Service and Promotions. This qualifies me to be actually called and regarded as an Anglophone Cameroonian; not someone who belongs neither West nor East of the River

Moungo. I'm now known to have come from the same tribe as the Honourable V.M, but not to have been aware of the fact until lately. He has stayed in the government for a long enough time to nominate whom he would like to succeed him. It is strange how God does his things! He certainly works in mysterious ways! Who could have imagined three years back that the Honourable V.M would choose me of all to succeed him? All this makes me feel the urgent need to sing God's praises; for he has shown that all is possible with him; that he might even raise the downtrodden: The "Damnés de la Terre" to such places of supremacy which they least imagined. Which confirms my strong conviction that our destinies are forged out in Heaven.

I kneel down to pray; I feel the need to. I close my eyes and allow my faith to wander away with my spirit. I search my mind for the most appropriate words of prayer. Only the following surface: "Lord, I have sinned and come short of thy glory. Forgive my transgressions and call me back to your right hand, that I might live faithfully ever after. Help me listen to thy voice inviting me to serve my country the more. May thy will be done. Amen."